'Short Stories' is a sparkling collection of tales from established writers and the UK's hottest new writing talent. Featuring stories from Meg Cabot, Melissa Nathan, Sophie Kinsella, Catherine Webb and many more, the book also showcases the winning entries of Waterstone's and Bliss Magazine's Teen Writing Competition 2004.

short stories

Meg Cabot
Sophie Kinsella
Melissa Nathan
Helen Olajumoke Oyeyemi
Chris Manby
Stella Duffy
plus many more

First published in Great Britain in 2004, Waterstone's, Capital Court,
Capital Interchange Way, Brentford, Middlesex, TW8 0EX.

All publication dates detailed in the author profiles relate to the publication
date of the paperback format of the related title, unless otherwise stated.

A CIP catalogue record for this book is available from the British Library.

ISBN (paperback) 1902603389

Cover image by David Oldfield

Set in 11/16pt Verdana
Typeset by Waterstone's, Brentford, Middlesex
in collaboration with the Dyslexia Institute
Printed and bound in Great Britain by Cox & Wyman Ltd, Reading, Berks

**THE DYSLEXIA
INSTITUTE**

All proceeds from the sale of this book will
go to the Dyslexia Institute

Introduction

Nearly 10% of the UK's population has some form of dyslexia, which causes difficulties in learning how to read, write and spell.

The Dyslexia Institute is an educational charity, founded in 1972, for the assessment and teaching of people with dyslexia and for the training of teachers. It has grown to become the only national dyslexia teaching organisation in the world.

In 2003 the Dyslexia Institute provided psychological assessments for over 7,500 children and adults; taught nearly 3,000 children and adults, and trained over 250 teachers on its postgraduate courses.

To continue their good work the Dyslexia Institute is dependent upon fees from assessments, tuition and training courses, and income from the sale of publications, fundraising and the generosity of benefactors. The Dyslexia Institute has become Waterstone's official charity and Waterstone's now works to raise awareness as well as to fundraise for the Dyslexia Institute.

This book has been produced in association with Bliss Magazine who, together with Waterstone's launched the Teen Writers Competition on World Book Day 2004 with the aim of discovering the country's newest writing talent. The winners of the competition have been published here alongside such acclaimed authors as Meg Cabot and Melissa Nathan.

The publication of this book is just one of the ways in which Waterstone's is helping the Dyslexia Institute and ALL proceeds of this book will go to the charity.

Waterstone's, Bliss and the Dyslexia Institute would like to extend their thanks to all the authors involved in this project and hope that it will inspire many more young writers, whatever their ability, to take up writing.

We hope you enjoy it!

Contents

The Teen Writers Competition Winners

Author profile
Meg Cabot

Meg Cabot's novels for teenagers have sold millions of copies around the world - and well over a million in the UK alone. She has lived in various parts of the US and in France, but now lives in New York City with her husband and one-eyed cat, Henrietta.

The latest book in the 'Princess Diaries' series, 'Sixsational', is to be published in October 2004.

'You Rock, Jen Greenley'
by Meg Cabot

I witnessed the kidnapping of Betty Ann Mulvaney.

Well, me and the twenty-three other people in first period Latin class at Clayton High School (student population 1,000).

Unlike everyone else, however, I actually did something to try to stop it. Well, sort of. I went, 'Kurt. What are you doing?'

Kurt just rolled his eyes. He was all, 'Relax, Jen. It's a joke, okay?'

But, see, there really isn't anything all that funny in the way Kurt Schraeder swiped Betty Ann from Mrs. Mulvaney's desk, then stuffed her into his Jansport. Some of her yellow yarn hair got caught in the teeth of his backpack's zipper, and everything.

Kurt didn't care. He just went right on zipping.

I should have said something more. I should have said,'Put her back, Kurt.'

Only I didn't.

Kurt was already high-fiving all of his friends, the other jocks who hang in the back row. They had to hide their smirks behind their workbooks when Mrs. Mulvaney came in after the second bell, a steaming cup of coffee in her hand.

'Good morning,' Mrs. Mulvaney sang.

Then she froze, her gaze going to the place on her desk where Betty Ann normally sat.

'Betty Ann?' Mrs. Mulvaney said, in this funny high-pitched voice...a voice that pierced my heart.

Because the thing is, Mrs. Mulvaney loves that stupid doll.

When Mrs. Mulvaney asked us if we'd seen Betty Ann, no one said anything. Because everyone— including me—is scared of Kurt. You just don't cross a guy like that. If Kurt Schraeder wants to kidnap a teacher's Cabbage Patch doll, you just let him, because otherwise you'll end up in a body cast.

'You don't think they're going to do anything to her, do you?' I asked my best friend Trina at lunch that day. 'What if they cut off her ear? And they send it to Mrs. M with a ransom note?'

'Oh my God,' Trina said. 'Would you get a grip? It's just a prank, okay? The seniors pull one every year.'

'It's just...' I couldn't get the picture of Betty Ann's yarny hair getting caught in that zipper out of my head. 'It just seems so wrong. Mrs. Mulvaney really loves that doll. I think...I think somebody should say something to Kurt.'

Trina rolled her eyes. 'Do you have a death wish?'

4

'Who's got a death wish?' Scott Bennet wanted to know, as he and his girlfriend Geri Lynn slid into chairs at our lunch table.

Trina pointed at me and said, 'Miss Jennifer Greenley here. She wants to try and get Betty Ann back from Kurt.'

'Ha,' Geri Lynn said. 'Been nice knowing you, Jen.'

Geri Lynn jiggled her can of Diet Coke as she spoke. Geri Lynn likes her Diet Coke flat, so she jiggles the can until it gets that way. But that isn't actually the weirdest thing about Geri Lynn. The weirdest thing about Geri Lynn–if you ask me, anyway–is that every time she and Scott make out in her parents' basement rec room, Geri draws a little heart in her datebook to mark the occasion.

I know this because she showed it to me once. Her datebook, I mean. There was a heart on like every single page.

Which is kind of funny. I mean that Geri and Scott are even going out. Because some people— like Trina, for instance—think Scott and I would make a better couple. On account of how he and I check out all the same books from the school library. Not that we've ever discussed this. It's just that whenever I go to check one of them out, Scott's signature is always there, right above mine, on the book's check-out card.

Trina says Scott might have asked me out, instead of Geri, if it wasn't for the fact that I'm so shy, I've barely ever even talked to him.

Still, I couldn't help noticing—the last time Geri opened her datebook—that lately, there haven't been all that many hearts in it.

'Jen's right,' was what Scott said, to my total and complete surprise. 'I know it's a prank. But pranks are supposed to be funny. And this one's just...not.'

Geri Lynn stopped jiggling her can.

'Hello,' she said. 'What do you care? It's just a stupid doll.'

'But Betty Ann isn't just a doll,' Scott said, echoing—as he seemed to do so often—my own feelings exactly. 'She's sort of like the unofficial school mascot. Kurt's gone too far this time. Somebody's got to do something.'

Geri rolled her eyes and went, 'Fine. You two try to get that stupid doll back. Don't expect me to come to your funerals.'

Which was how I ended up in the front seat of Scott Bennet's beat up old Audi later that afternoon, on Operation Rescue Betty Ann Mulvaney.

'So,' he wanted to know. 'What's the plan?'

Yeah. I would have liked to know the same thing. The problem was, I didn't have one. All I'd been able to think about, since the moment Scott

6

had said he'd help me get Betty Ann back, was that this must mean he likes me. I mean, at least a little. As a friend.

Which might explain why my palms were so sweaty all of a sudden.

'Um,' I said. 'I guess the plan is...we go to his house? I know he was heading home after school. I overheard him telling some guys he'd meet them at the lake.'

'Sounds good,' Scott said, and made the turn onto Sycamore, Kurt's street. 'But what, exactly, are we going to do then? Break in and take her? Shouldn't we wait until dark? Get some night-vision goggles?'

'Funny,' I said. 'Just drive.'

When we pulled up to Kurt's house, his Grand Am wasn't in the driveway.

'So,' Scott said, as he pulled into the driveway and switched the ignition off. 'What now?'

'I don't know,' I said. 'I guess...we see if it's here? The doll, I mean. I doubt he took her to the lake with him.'

Scott followed me up the steps to the Schraeders' front door. I hoped he couldn't see how hard my heart was beating beneath my T-shirt. The truth was, I was totally nervous. My stomach hurt. My hands were still all sweaty–but not because I was afraid of Kurt.

The door was opened by Kurt's little sister. Her

7

name, according to the gold necklace she wore, was Vicky.

Scott and I exchanged glances. Then, before he could say a word, I dropped my hands down to my knees (which was good, because then I could wipe the sweat off on my jeans) so that my gaze was level with hers and said, 'Hi! Is your brother home?'

Vicky pulled the braid tip she'd been sucking on out of her mouth and went, 'No. He went to the lake.'

'Oh, no,' I said, trying to look disappointed. 'Well, did he leave something for me? A doll?'

Vicky's eyes grew even wider. 'You mean Betty Ann?'

'Yes,' I said, brightly. 'Betty Ann. See, it's my turn to look after her. Betty Ann, I mean. I guess Kurt forgot. Could you do me a favour? Could you run and get her for me?'

Back went the tip of the braid into the mouth.

'I'm not allowed to go in Kurt's room,' Vicky said, as she sucked energetically. 'He said if I did it again, he'd pound me.'

'Oh, he won't mind this one time, Vicky,' I said. 'In fact, you'll be doing him a huge favour. Because you see, if I don't get Betty Ann back, and right this very minute, someone is going to go to the school principal and tell him that Kurt's the one who took Betty Ann in the first place,

8

and then Kurt probably won't get to graduate.'

The braid dropped from Vicky's mouth. 'Someone would do that?'

'Oh, yes,' I said. 'Someone would. So you see, you'd really be helping Kurt if you could do this one little thing for me.'

'Okay,' Vicky said, with a shrug. 'I'll be right back.'

She took off. When I glanced at Scott, he was shaking his head at me...but there was a smile on his lips.

'What happened to you?' he wanted to know.

'What do you mean?' I asked, a little alarmed.

'You never used to be like this,' Scott said. 'You used to...I don't know. Be kind of shy. This is the most I've heard you talk...ever.'

I couldn't believe he'd noticed. I mean, that he'd been paying attention.

To me.

'I don't know,' I said, looking away so he wouldn't see that I was blushing. 'I guess I just decided to take a stand.'

'I'll say,' Scott said.

We heard running footsteps, and then Vicky reappeared, Betty Ann in her arms.

'Here she is,' Vicky said, handing the doll over. 'I found her under Kurt's bed.'

'Thanks, Vicky,' I said, tucking Betty Ann beneath my arm. 'You're the best. 'Bye!' Vicky called, and waved as we hurried down the steps to Scott's car.

Once we were a safe distance from Sycamore, Scott glanced at me and said, 'That was the coolest thing I've ever seen. You rock, Jen Greenley.'

It wasn't a heart in a datebook.

But I couldn't help feeling like it was a start.

Author profile
Cathy Cassidy

'I think I've always loved books and as soon as I could write was scribbling stories. When I was thirteen I was given a second-hand typewriter and began to bash out short stories for my favourite teen magazine. I must have sent dozens off, and I got dozens of very polite, encouraging rejections in return!'

Born in 1962, Cathy's CV is varied. She has been the editor of Jackie magazine, an art teacher, a freelance writer and an agony aunt! She lives in Galloway in Scotland.

Her first book 'Dizzy' was published in June 2004.

The Journey
by Cathy Cassidy

I once knew a boy called Chip McCorcoran who travelled all the way from Penny Lane to Liverpool Coach Station on rollerblades, to wave goodbye to his girlfriend. He travelled through Sefton Park and Princes Park, skated right through Toxteth and past the two cathedrals, then cruised down Mount Pleasant, grabbing up a few lanky tulips on the way. He gave his girlfriend a kiss and a hug, offered her the tulips and waved as the coach rumbled away from the kerb, taking her to a fortnight of sun, sand and freedom on the Cornish coast.

It was the most romantic gesture I've ever seen, and I should know. I was the girl on the coach.

Sadly, I was only 14 at the time, and I blushed pure purple when Chip bowled up at the coach station, skidding into a 180 degree turn and kissing me on the lips right under the noses of my mum, dad and little sister.

'Chip!' I muttered, horrified. 'Don't! People are looking!'

'And?' Chip had replied. 'People are looking. So what?'

He handed me three wilting tulips, two of which had the roots still attached. Damp soil rained down on my pink embroidered combats.

'Sweet,' said Kelly, my little sister, who had a bit of crush on Chip.

'They're nicked, aren't they?' I said, thinking of the neat council flower beds dotted around the city centre.

'Not nicked, liberated,' Chip corrected me.

'Nicked,' I said.

I guess I just didn't appreciate Chip back then. Dad loaded our suitcases into the luggage hold and we climbed onto the coach, and I smiled and blushed and pulled faces at Chip through the window as we waited for the coach to start.

I looked at Chip, a grinning skater-goth sipping Coke on the kerbside and blowing kisses, and I wished he was different. I wished he was tall, cool, the kind of lad who wore designer jeans, not a black beanie hat, a crumpled t-shirt and tattered combats. I wished he was the kind of boy who travelled by car or by motorbike, not rollerblades. I wanted red roses, not mangled tulips. I dreamed of posh restaurants and swanky clubs, but all I got were nights hanging out at the skate park or huddled in a garage listening to his rackety band practice, and, on a Saturday, a

14

shared slice of pizza at the cafe in Quiggins.

I didn't know then that a lad who would skate for miles to give you a kiss and a flower before you went on holiday was something so special, so magical, it might never happen again. It was love, and I threw it away.

I went to Cornwall and loafed around on the beach and I didn't think of Chip, not one little bit.

I flirted with the surfer boys, and in the last week I hooked up with a lad called Marty with sun-bleached blond hair and skin the colour of honey. We went to beach barbies and discos and we walked along the sand in the moonlight and kissed while the surf curled in around our feet.

Marty was cool. He liked the same music I liked, and didn't try to make me listen to loud, jangly bands I'd never heard of, like The Rasmus and Less Than Jake and Good Charlotte. He wore cute board shorts on the beach, but when he dressed up he looked like a Greek god in pale linen chinos and soft white shirts that showed off his tan.

He knew how to surf, he knew how to dance, he knew how to kiss. He was just about perfect, but not quite. There was something wrong, something askew, and it took me the whole week to figure it out.

He was cool, he was fun, but he just wasn't Chip.

I said goodbye to Marty and thanked him for a lovely week, but neither of us exchanged addresses. It had been a holiday romance, and maybe, for me, a chance to do some growing up and sort out what I wanted in life. I knew it wasn't Marty.

Things with Chip would be different from now on, I decided. I'd appreciate him more, learn to like his music, admire his skills on guitar and rollerblades. I couldn't wait to see his lopsided grin, his soft green eyes, that scuddy old beanie hat jammed down over floppy dark hair.

He came round the day after we got back from Cornwall. I heard him arrive, turning a perfect kick-flip on the garden path with his skateboard, and waved out of my bedroom window. I should have just run down the stairs to give him a hug, but I wanted to make a good impression. Maybe I was still feeling guilty about Marty.

I took a few minutes in front of the dressing table mirror, dragging black eyeliner around my eyes to look more rock-chick, mussing up my hair so it wouldn't look like I'd just spent a whole hour straightening it.

When I walked into the sitting room, Chip was sitting with my little sister on the sofa, looking through the batch of holiday snaps she'd had developed earlier that day. He was grinning, laughing at the picture of me in my bikini, admiring the wobbly scenic views of the surf beach.

'Who's that, then?' he asked.

I went cold. I wanted to run over to the sofa and grab the photos and rip them into tiny shreds, but I was stuck there in the doorway, my face a perfect mask of guilt and alarm. I willed Kelly to look up at me, to understand, to do a cover-up if it was needed. She didn't even notice I was there.

'Oh, that's Marty,' she answered easily. 'He was this really cool surfer guy that Sara dated in Cornwall.'

I watched as Kelly suddenly realised what she'd said. Her face flushed pink, then scarlet. Her hand flew to her mouth, and her eyes widened in horror.

'Yeah?' said Chip. 'That's interesting.'

His voice was cold, and so were his eyes when they locked onto mine. He stood up, letting the photograph flutter to the carpet. It was one I didn't even know Kelly had taken, of Marty carrying his surfboard and grinning at the camera.

'No,' Kelly said, panicking. 'What am I saying? Not Sara. He was dating this girl called Cara, that's right...'

'Don't bother, Kelly,' Chip said kindly. 'It's OK. I don't know why I'm even surprised.'

17

He looked at me, and I opened my mouth to explain, to protest, to plead, but the words just wouldn't come. I saw the hurt in his soft green eyes and it was all I could do to blink back the tears and swallow the ache in my throat. He pushed past me, out of the front door. He picked up his skateboard from the garden path, threw it down on the kerbside and rattled off along the street. I watched him go until the tears blurred my vision and I sat down on the doorstep and cried and cried and cried.

That was over a year ago. I'm older, maybe wiser. I know now what it was that I threw away, and I'll have to live with that knowledge forever. Chip loved me and I threw it all back in his face. I lost the only lad I really wanted, and I did it in style.

I still see Chip, sometimes. I've seen him date other girls, and felt the hurt wrap around my heart like barbed wire. He's older than me, and I've watched him sit A levels and get the grades he wanted, the college place he dreamed about. Chip is going to music college in Glasgow.

Last night, there was a big party at Chip's place so he could say goodbye to everyone.

'Please come,' Chip's mate, Joe, said when he asked me. 'Chip would love to see you. He still talks about you, y'know.'

'I don't think so,' I stalled. 'It ended pretty badly.'

'So maybe this would be a chance to set things straight, wish him luck, tie up those loose ends?' Joe suggested. 'He's taking the nine-thirty train on Sunday morning, but he won't let any of us go to the station to see him off, not mates, not family, nobody. The party'll be your last chance to say goodbye. Please come. For Chip?'

So I went to the party. I watched my ex-boyfriend dancing to those crashy, clashy bands and talking to his friends. He still looked young and crumpled and couldn't-care-less, with his soft green eyes and his lopsided grin. Everyone was wishing him luck, telling him to work hard, keep in touch, remember them when he's famous.

He saw me, and his grin flickered and died.

'Sara,' he said, 'Hi. I'm glad you came.'

'I just wanted to say...'

But whatever I wanted to say was lost, because a big posse of Year 12 girls swooped down and dragged him away to dance, and I slipped away soon after that.

I wanted to say good luck, and goodbye, and most of all I wanted to say sorry, but last night was not the time or the place to do it.

Chip McCorcoran is as cool as homemade vanilla ice cream and as hot as cappucino with chocolate sprinkles, and he still owns a huge chunk of my heart. I can't let him go away without telling him that, can I? It's too late for what I want to say, but suddenly I know that I have to say it all the same. Better late than never.

I grab my jacket and scoop up the bulky carrier bag from the hallway, and start walking. I walk through Sefton Park, past the lakes and the flowerbeds and the grass, then on through Princes Park. I keep thinking I'll catch a bus on the boulevard, but nothing comes along until I'm way up by the Anglican cathedral and it's just not worth it by that time. I march on along Rodney Street until I see the spiky wigwam of the Catholic cathedral, then turn down the hill towards Lime Street Station.

The Glasgow train is running on time, and I have just minutes to spare. I sit on a bench and change my shoes, stuffing my feet into Kelly's rollerblades which are two sizes too small and slightly soggy from being left out in the rain overnight. I try to stand upright, tottering and pink-faced. It's like standing on razor-blades. I take a deep breath and start out towards the flower stall, stopping to buy a bunch of red and white daisies. I'd have liked tulips, but it's September, and there are none to be had anywhere.

The guard doesn't want to let me through onto the platform, so I have to explain about Chip and the party and how I have to apologise, right now, before it's all too late. He lets me through.

The last few people are getting onto the train, but I can't see Chip anywhere. I skate along the platform, slowly, painfully, carrying the red and white daisies. I scan every window, every carriage, and there, in the last one, is Chip. His face lights up with shock, and I can't tell if he's pleased or horrified.

He clambers to his feet and scoots along to the doorway, dragging down the window so we can talk.

'Sara,' he says. 'You came to say goodbye.'

I shove the flowers at him.

'Goodbye and good luck, but mainly sorry,' I tell him. 'I'm sorry for the way I treated you. I made a mega mistake, Chip, and I'll never forgive myself for that. I wish I could undo what happened, but I can't. All I can do is say sorry. I know it's too late, but...'

'Is it?' Chip asks.

'Is it what?'

'Too late?'

He looks at me with those soft green eyes and the guard walks along the platform shouting at everyone to stand clear. The whistle blows.

'Hang on,' says Chip. He hauls open the door, chucking bags and rucksacks out onto the platform. A skateboard follows, and rollerblades, and his big electric guitar and amp. The train is pulling away as Chip jumps down and slams the door.

'You'll miss it,' I say, bewildered.

'There's another one,' Chip says. 'Later.'

We sit down on a bench with Chip's possessions piled up in a mound beside us.

'You didn't skate the whole way here, did you?' he asks, looking at the borrowed rollerblades.

'No, just along the platform,' I admit. 'They're way too small, and I'm rubbish, anyway. Sorry I couldn't get tulips,' I add, stroking one of the daisies.

'These are bought, aren't they?' Chip says sternly.

'Not bought, liberated...' I say.

'Definitely bought.'

He leans over to kiss me, right there on the bench where everyone can see.

'Chip!' I protest. 'People are looking!'

'And?' he laughs. 'People are looking. So what?'

'So kiss me again,' I say, and he does.

Author profile
Echo Freer

Echo Freer was born and brought up in Yorkshire. After training to be a teacher she moved to London where she taught special needs in one of London's social priority areas. When her son was diagnosed as severely dyslexic, she completed a specialist training to teach and diagnose specific learning difficulties. She now assesses and teaches under-achieving children in a special unit attached to one of London's teaching hospitals. She lives in London with her son.

Her latest novel, 'Blaggers', features the daughter of an Essex gangster, Mercedes Bent and was published in May 2004.

The Scream

by Echo Freer

The clock on the dashboard clicked on to midnight as Davey swung the car off the main road and into the lane that led to the village. Mum was going to go ballistic. In fact that's probably the understatement of the decade. A neutron bomb makes less noise than my mum when she loses it, especially if I happen to be within a ten-mile radius!

I could probably come up with a pretty good defence against the first charge, which would be 'staying out later than I was allowed'. I'd been given strict instructions to be home by ten thirty but, be honest, how many fifteen-year-olds have to be home by half past ten in the school holidays? And anyway, what did she think was going to happen to me, stuck out in the wilds? Or should I say, the tames, because wild it certainly isn't round here.

We'd moved out of town three months ago to this village that is so far out in the sticks it makes 'the sticks' look like twigs on some distant horizon. It was supposed to be so that we could make a new start after Dad died, but new starts like this are about as welcome as foot and mouth disease. The place is full of yokels and coffin dodgers.

There's only one other person of my age in the whole village who is remotely cool, which brings me to the second and much more serious charge Mum is likely to bring against me: Davey.

'So what did you tell the iron lady you were doing tonight?' Davey asked.

'Careful!' I said, as the car skidded and I was thrown against the passenger door. It wasn't long since he'd passed his test and he'd taken the corner a bit too fast.

'Ooooo! Is little Miss Townie scared?' he tormented, deliberately swerving the car from side to side as he sped down the narrow country road.

'Scared? Yeah right!' I must confess, I felt a bit uneasy, but I tried to cover it. 'I told her I was cycling over to Kelly's,' I said, trying to get the conversation back on track. Kelly's this nerdy girl who lives in a bungalow on the main road and I was about as likely to go to see her as I would be to do aqua-aerobics in the village duck pond.

Davey threw back his head and laughed. 'And she bought it?' He shook his head in disbelief. 'Jeez! Your old woman is more stupid than I realised.'

And that was the turning point for me. I mean, Mum can be a pain in the bum sometimes but I was getting sick of his insults.

'My mum is not stupid,' I said defensively.

'Come on – you cycle up to the main road?' he snorted. 'Get real!'

'Durr! Not everyone is old enough to drive,' I snapped back. 'How do you think I get over to your house? On jet-skis?'

Davey lives in a cottage about half a mile outside the village and buses in this neck of the woods run once a day into town and once a day back again – end of! Miss the bus and there'll be another along in twenty-four hours. If this was civilisation, I was a Neanderthal. So, like it or lump it, I had no option but to take to a pair of wheels whenever I wanted to escape.

'OK, OK – keep your hair on!' Davey jeered.

We'd been going out for about a month but he was starting to get up my nose – not that I was going to tell Mum. She'd deemed Davey totally off limits the minute we moved in. Not just because he was two years older than me, but also because the old biddies in the Women's Institute had told her that he'd got into some trouble when he was younger. Nothing heavy; just a bit of bunking off and shoplifting – it didn't bother me. What was bothering me now though, was him dissing my mum and me, so I folded my arms and stared straight ahead.

The hedges on either side of the lane were very high so that at times it was like driving through a tunnel.

'You sulking now?' he asked, but I didn't answer. 'Oh very mature, I'm sure. I should've known better than to go out with a little kid,' he ridiculed. Then he started turning the steering wheel like a maniac again so that the car veered from one side of the road to the other.

'Pack it in!' I said.

But he didn't. I was starting to get really annoyed – plus, there was a distinct chance that I might chuck any minute. Then, suddenly, as we rounded a sharp bend, I saw a red light bobbing along the lane in front of us.

'Davey, slow down – there's someone on a bike.'

But he didn't slow down and the closer we got the more clearly I could see that the person on the bike was my brother, Sam. He was a year older than I was and since Dad had died he seemed to have assumed the role of man-of-the-house, which was *soooo* irritating. You'd think he was sixty instead of sixteen.

'What's ferret-face doing out this late?' Davey jeered.

'Probably out looking for me.'

How humiliating was that? It wasn't like I was a

little kid any more and yet Mum must have sent Sam over to Kelly's. How was I ever going to live that down?

'Well, let's give him a bit of a fright, shall we?' Davey laughed, steering the car towards the bike.

'No!' Sam might be a bit of a pilchard but he was my brother.

'If you don't like my driving, you can get out and walk,' Davey threatened, putting his foot down and heading straight for the bike. Sam turned his head and we were so close that I could see him squinting as the car headlights shone into his eyes.

'Don't be so stupid!' I grabbed the steering wheel and tried to steer the car away from the bike. But, as the car swerved, I saw Sam wobble and he seemed to fall. It all happened in slow motion and I could see Sam's expression of horror as his bike toppled to the left and he went up into the air right in front of the car.

'Stop!' I screamed.

And, hallelujah, for once Davey actually did as I asked and slammed on the brakes. But the car skidded and slewed sideways so violently that my head cracked against the window.

'Oh!' I moaned as I sat up, rubbing my head. Then shouted at Davey, 'You moron!'

But when I looked round, I was gobsmacked; Davey had only driven off and left me! I must have blacked out when my head hit the glass and the weasel had done what he'd threatened and put me out of the car to walk home. I couldn't believe it. What a rat! In fact, calling him a rat was an insult to rodents the world over. I was fuming! And then I remembered Sam. I hoped he was all right. I ran back to where my brother had fallen off but I couldn't see him.

'Sam!' I called, but there was no reply.

I started to feel anxious. What if Sam had been knocked unconscious too and was lying in the hedgerow somewhere? Luckily it was a full moon so the light was quite bright. I walked slowly along the grass verge looking for either Sam or his bike but there was no sign of either. Now I was really worried. Perhaps we'd skidded further than I thought, so I walked almost the entire length of the lane, scouring the hedgerows. But there was still nothing: no skid marks, no bits of bicycle metal, no blood, no torn clothing. It was as though Sam had never even been there. I was starting to freak out.

Then it occurred to me – he was probably playing some kid's trick and hiding in the bushes. Of course! I bet he was really peed off when Mum told him to go looking for me and this was his way of getting his own back. Well, ha ha ha, because the joke was on him now. No way was I going to spend the night pandering to his warped sense of humour. I was in for enough aggro as it was but if I went home now, then Sam'd be the one with the explaining to do.

As I walked home I tried to brace myself for the full-scale eruption from Mum. There was no point in even trying to think up an excuse; I was just going to have to front this one out. But as I got out my keys, something seemed weird. Normally Mum would be sitting up waiting for me and she'd thunder downstairs like a pre-menstrual rhino the second my key hit the lock – but not tonight; everything was in darkness. And even more creepy was that once I was inside I could see that Sam's bike was in the hall. I couldn't believe it! I'd spent half the night (OK, well at least half an hour) scouring the lane for him when he hadn't even had the decency to hang around long enough to check that I was OK after we'd skidded. And to think, I'd actually been worried about him for about a millisecond. I swore I would kill Sam for that.

I crept upstairs as quietly as I could. Ever since Dad died, Mum and Sam had taken to sleeping with their bedroom doors open – don't ask me why. I peeked in and, sure enough, there they were – both sparko. At least it gave me some breathing space before I had to face them in the morning.

It was late when I woke and I could hear

31

activity downstairs. I wondered how long I could put off going down and discovering that I'd been found guilty in my absence and sentenced to ten years' hard labour in Mum's vegetable patch.

Mum's voice called upstairs. 'Sam! You ready yet?'

There was a grunt from my brother's room.

'Come on, love,' she said, softly. 'We need to go. People are starting to arrive.'

Arrive? For what? I wondered. Was there something that I'd forgotten about? To be honest, I hadn't been at home much this holiday, so it was more than likely that I'd missed out on some gossip, although I was more concerned with the fact that no one had been on my case about getting home late. That was distinctly strange – maybe whatever was happening today had taken precedence over my nocturnal activities. Or maybe I was in such trouble that no one was speaking to me. Yes, that was more likely – I was being given the cold shoulder. Well, I could handle that. Being sent to Coventry was better than being given a load of grief.

I heard Sam go downstairs and then the front door shut. Phew! I seemed to have got away with it for the moment.

I thought that while they were out, I'd take the opportunity to walk over to Davey's and pick up my bike. Then I'd dump him. Last night had shown me what a jerk he really was and, although I hate to admit it, Mum was probably right about him – not that I would ever let her know that!

Our house is right opposite the village church and as I left, I noticed masses of people milling around. Normally the vicar's lucky to pull in half a dozen on a Sunday, so it was bizarre that the place was full to bursting in the middle of the week. Curiosity got the better of me, and I went across to have a nose about – just find out what was happening. Maybe, I thought, there was someone famous coming to the village and Mum hadn't told me because she wanted to punish me.

People were filing in, so I joined them, peering about to see if I could catch a glimpse of anything remotely interesting. I saw Mum and Sam standing at the back and the strangest thing was, Sam had a black eye and a cut on his lip! So he had been injured last night. Sam used to be an OK guy; it's all this Dad's mini-me stuff that's got up my nose recently. So I suddenly felt a twinge of guilt

I went over to them. 'Oh my God, Sam – I'm really sorry. Are you OK?'

But he completely ignored me. Brilliant! I mean, that's the thanks I get for apologising. Although I suppose part of me could understand him being peed off. If I'd been back on time, he wouldn't have had to go out looking for me. But there's no excuse for freezing me out – or leaving me alone in the lane.

I looked at Mum, sheepishly. 'Look, I'm sorry about last night, OK?'

But she didn't want to know either. She just folded her arms and turned away. Did I say the cold shoulder was better than being given a load of grief? Well, forget it. But if that was how they wanted to play it, let them have it their way. I wasn't going to hang around – it was probably just some boring village meeting anyway.

I was just about to leave when Mum shouted, 'How dare you?' Which, to be honest, I thought was a bit off. I mean, I'm not religious or anything, but even so, to shout in a church? 'Get out! Just get out!' she screamed.

At first, I was shocked. OK, so I know I haven't exactly been an angel since Dad died and maybe I've given her more headaches than a migraine clinic but having a go at me in public was a bit too much. And, after all, I had said I was sorry – twice!

But then I realised that she wasn't shouting at me; she was looking past me towards the doorway. I wasn't sure which was worse – being shouted at in front of everyone or being ignored again. Anyway, I turned round to see who'd been on the receiving end and there in the entrance to the church was Davey. Only he was in a wheelchair with his leg in plaster and his face was all cut.

'Davey!' I couldn't believe it. I looked from my brother to my boyfriend (well, ex – but he didn't know it yet). 'What the hell happened last night after I'd hit my head? Did you two have some sort of fight?'

Neither of them spoke. They just glared at each other and then Mum lurched towards Davey. Everyone else was staring. It was eerily quiet in there with this creepy organ music playing in the background.

'Leave him alone, Mum,' Sam said, trying to restrain her.

Then Davey spoke, 'It wasn't my fault, honestly. She just grabbed the wheel. I couldn't do anything.'

'What?' I was feeling distinctly confused. 'Who grabbed the wheel? Davey, who are you talking about?' My head was spinning. I was starting to feel queasy. I had to get out. I needed some air.

At the back of the church was a wall-mounted magazine rack with religious periodicals and parish newsletters. As I began to push my way out, the front page of the local newspaper caught my eye. There was a photograph of me on it.

I stopped and stared, hardly able to believe what I was seeing. Next to it was a picture of a car – Davey's car, lying in a ditch like a turtle that had gone belly up. The headline read: Village mourns teenage crash victim. What village? What teenage crash victim? Everything was swimming. This wasn't true – it must be some sort of hideous nightmare.

Four men in suits appeared in the doorway, carrying a coffin on their shoulders. An icy shudder of realisation ran the length of my spine.

'Nooooooo!' I screamed. 'I'm here! I'm alive!'

There must have been a terrible mistake. I stood in front of them, blocking their path. But they walked right through me.

'Mum!' I yelled. 'I'm sorry. Look – I'm here!'

Mum and Sam looked neither left nor right as they followed the pallbearers. I ran to the front of the church. They were ignoring me. Everyone was ignoring me.

'Heeeeelp!' It was imperative that someone heard me before it was too late.

Then a voice whispered in my ear, 'It's all right, love. I'm here.'

A flood of relief coursed through me. Thank heavens! Someone had heard me. And it was a voice I recognised; a voice that had sung me to sleep when I was little.

'Dad?'

'You can come with me now,' he said, softly.

'But...' I was feeling confused again. It couldn't

be Dad; Dad was dead.

I looked from one parent to the other. Mum was alive and I was alive – I had to be. I had so much more to do; so much more life to live.

'Come with me,' Dad coaxed, gently.

'No,' I cried. 'This isn't happening. I'm not dead.' I looked back at Mum. 'Tell him,' I pleaded but my voice seemed to be getting fainter.

A mist was clouding my eyes and I felt as though I was being drawn gently upwards away from the ceremony in the church below, away from Mum and Sam.

'NOOOoooooooo!' I gave one final scream before they petered into oblivion.

Author profile
Catherine Webb

With four novels already in print at the age of 18, Catherine Webb has quickly established herself as one of the most talented and exciting young writers in the UK.

Her next novel,'The Extraordinary and Unusual Adventures of Horatio Lyle', the story of a Victorian sleuth with a passion for science and inventions, was written in between physics and history 'A' level classes and will be published in November 2005.

The Phone Call
by Catherine Webb

'You have reached Dr Wendle's office. I'm afraid I'm not in at the moment, but please leave your message after the tone. Thank you.'

'Dr Wendle? It's me. I mean, obviously it's me, but that's not very helpful, it's the guy you met yesterday. You know, you were in the lift, we got stuck while evacuating the building, you said you were a psychiatrist, I said I needed help, you took one of my smokes and... is there a time limit on these things? I mean, you don't just cut off your callers, do you, just mid...'

'You have reached Dr Wendle's office. I'm afraid I'm not in at the moment, but please leave your message after the tone. Thank you.'

'... sentence. Hello? Hello?! Hell, I'm really depressed. People hate me, really hate me, I get blamed for everything and everyone's problems, it's sometimes like God really does hate me, like it's my fault humankind's weak and everything...'

'Hello?'

'Hello, Dr Wendle, is that you?'

39

'This is Dr Wendle. Who am I talking to?'

'I'm the guy you met in the lift yesterday. The building was burning, and...'

'I remember yesterday. How can I help you? What's your name?'

'Call me Sam.'

'Is that what everyone calls you?'

'No, it's more like 'Devil' or the like - unimaginative crap. But Sam has a ring.'

'Do you want to remain anonymous?'

'I just think you might hate me, I don't want this relationship to start on the wrong foot...'

'I'm not going to hate you Sam. Did anyone recommend me to you?'

'No. You just stuck me as having a good soul.'

'Look, Sam, I'd love to talk to you, but I think you really ought to make an appointment...'

'You're just going to leave me? I might be standing on the edge of a building about to jump!'

'Are you, Sam?'

'Well, no, not right now, but you wouldn't know. How'd you feel if you were hated by everyone? Or are you?'

'Are you saying that you're feeling suicidal tendencies?'

'Did you hear me say that? Do you think I'm suicidal? Great, now I really feel depressed. I'll go and find a gas oven somewhere...'

'Don't do that. Talk to me, Sam. Calmly. Tell me what's upsetting you.'

'You mean it?'

'If you'd prefer to come and meet face to face I have a slot available...'

'No, no, I just want to talk! You'd probably take one look at me and refuse to speak to me ever again.'

'Do you feel uncomfortable as a person, Sam?'

'Not usually, but you know, it's just the stares you get. After the 1960s I thought people would be more accepting, more open, more understanding. You ever see that film... oh, 1980s, very cool, lots of hair... not Invasion of the Body Snatchers... but you know the thing with the big hair? I thought that if I got myself a hair-do like that I could go anywhere and no one would comment, no one would notice. But people scream at me.'

'Does this upset you?'

'Wouldn't it upset you?'

'I suppose it would. But if you don't feel comfortable with the reactions of people perhaps it's because you don't feel comfortable with the image you project. What do you do?'

'What, hobbies?'

'If you like.'

'I play golf.'

'Do you find that satisfying?'

'It's alright.'

'Is it a social occasion? Do you feel comfortable in the company of other golfers?'

'Hell yeah! They're all lawyers and senior execs and the like, they say anything to me that I want, in the hope of a quick cash pay-out at the end of the day, eternal damnation be damned!'

'They flatter you?'

'Doc, everyone flatters me at some point or another.'

'Is that it? Is it the superficiality of their reactions that upsets you?'

'Flattery's fine.'

'You must be a very senior figure, Sam.'

'Oh yeah. I've eaten from the tree of knowledge.'

'Are you married?'

'The girls just don't fall for me. Well, the ones with the tentacles and the drink problems and bad skin, they don't mind me. But the bimbos? They come round eventually, but usually only after they've committed murder or something.'

'Forgive the personal nature of this question, but do you have an... active love-life, Sam?'

'I wouldn't call it love. Hell, the word burns just to say it. But sure, like I said, everyone comes round to me eventually. Except for the lollipop ladies.'

'Lollipop ladies?'

'Yeah. It's a bugger, isn't it?'

'Where are you from, Sam? Are you American?'

'American? Only spiritually.'

'What does that mean? 'Only spiritually'?'

'The entire market economy they've got - the continent is practically eating out of my palm. I always like to say I've got a monopoly on the American soul, but in fairness it's probably only a controlling interest.'

'You're in business? Banking, investment?'

'All of them.'

'Do you have much time outside your business hours for recreation and socialising?'

'Not really. It's a 24/7, eternity kind of job.'

'Do you want a family?'

'I can't change nappies.'

'That's something you can learn, though?'

'Yeah, but nappies. And what if I woke up one day and discovered the kid had hit puberty, grown a tail, found a pitch fork and moved to LA? I'd go mental. It'd make St Helens look like a little geological fart.'

'Do you like children?'

'Little buggers.'

'Why do you feel that way, Sam? Tell me about your childhood?'

'My childhood? My childhood? Beloved of God, I was! Played the sodding harp, lived in the crystal towers, eternal bliss, my childhood!'

'Sam, this really would be easier if you'd come down, meet eye to eye, have a few...'

'No. Really. You aren't going to like me.'

'Why do you think that?'

'You like iguanas?'

'I don't really see the....'

'Just answer the question, doc.'

'Well, no, not particularly.'

'You like squid? You know, those big pink ones that come out of the deep and gobble up ships in bad horror films of a certain vintage?'

'Well, no, not that kind of squid....'

'How'd you feel about methane?'

'Pardon?'

'Methane? How'd you feel about it?'

'I never really had an emotional reaction. But I suppose it's a health hazard and therefore...'

'You wouldn't like me.'

'You don't feel that you might be doing yourself down, do you, Sam?'

'Modesty isn't a deadly sin, doc. I mean, take a guy like you. Where'd you study for this job?'

'It's really not important...'

'Go on, just answer the question.'

'Well, if you must know, I went to Yale.'

'And?'

'And? And do you want to see my certificate?'

'Tell me how you graduated.'

'I am fully qualified.'

'You were top of your class, doc. Commended by the faculty and everything. If I were you, I'd be advertising this.'

'I'm very impressed that you know this, Sam, but I would like to know...'

'Tell me about your family.'

'What?'

'Go on, doc. Tell me about your family.'

'Well... I have a wife and two sons.'

'And?'

'And? We live happily and comfortably.'

'You aren't afraid that your wife might be going with someone else?'

'No, not at all, and, Sam, I really don't think that this is relevant to your...'

'You're not worried that she might be going with someone called Russell? Six foot four, goes to the gym, like a rural hunky adonis only on six figures a year and no decimal point?'

'Sam, I don't know what you're implying but...'

'Hey, if you want to be reasonable, that's your call. But you see my point, right?'

'Let's talk about you, not me. Let me ask this - what at this exact moment, now, are you looking at, and how does it make you feel?'

'The decor.'

'Describe it.'

'Well... there's my desk, that's fine. You know, I've got one of those clicky metal things, where you hit one and the other at the other end starts swinging in a perpetual motion type thing....'

'I know the thing. I've got one on my desk, in fact.'

'Really? That's a sure sign of sexual repression, doc.'

'You think so?'

'Sure! What colour socks are you wearing now?'

'Pardon?'

'Go on. Tell me.'

'I'm wearing red socks...'

'Oh, doc.'

'Sam, I think we're straying from the issue. What else is upsetting you about your surroundings?'

'Well... the wall is irritating. It's got this arty jagged-rock, pitted-pitch thing going for it which was really hip in 1300 but now is very out of fashion completely. And there's this brimstone thing in the corner that was therapeutic once but now just keeps on packing up every month. You know how much these repair people charge? Retrain as a plumber, doc, you'll be living in fortune forever.'

'And what can you see out of your window?'

'The nether circle of hell.'

'You're not based in Manhattan, are you?'

'I wanted to be, but couldn't cope with the

rent. This is more like fiery pitch, screaming tormented souls, you know the thing.'

'Do you find that your working environment affects your mood, Sam?'

'What'd you think?'

'I want to hear your view.'

'Well... it's alright. You know? I mean, sure, it's not the balmy airs of Elysium or the bright sunlit uplands of Paradise, but it's okay. It's got charms.'

'Do you enjoy travel?'

'Nah.'

'No?'

'Nah. Got bored long time ago. Seen one civilization's corrupt evil practices, seen them all.'

'Do you believe that as an absolute?'

'What?'

'I mean.... do you believe that all civilizations share the same tendency towards corruption?'

'Of course they do! They might not be sacrificing people on stone altars openly now, but that's only because they've invented taxation and the IRS! I mean, doc, let me ask you this, plainly - how do you feel about the state of your immortal soul? If you were to be hit by a frozen ready meal packet falling from a plane at about 4.38 p.m. tomorrow evening while you're waiting at the bus stop for the 34C back to your wife and collapse from internal brain damage on the way to hospital while a guy called Bob was trying to work out where he'd put the plasma, what would you be reincarnated as? Genius astronaut who discovers gold on Mars, or toilet brush? It'll help me trust you, help me open up in this entire process.'

'Truly... I don't believe in reincarnation.'

'But you believe in heaven and hell, right?'

'I suppose, in a way, I do believe...'

'So which do you think it's going to be? The halls of your ancestors drinking the ambrosia of the gods, or the fiery screaming? Come on, if you've only got twenty four... no, twenty three hours and fifty two minutes.... left to live?'

'I suppose it all depends on what you believe justifies your existence.'

'Uh-huh. And what justifies yours?'

'I beg your pardon?'

'What reason do you have for living?'

'I...I am a doctor, I help people and...'

'Help people? Hell, doc, I'm about to go and stick my head in the oven and you say you're here to help people? Do you know how much money this conversation is costing? I got the Freepay package for long-distant calls, but it's only for calls over twenty minutes duration and I don't know if I have the willpower to last that long! You take people's cash, you take it from the first moment they call you, and then you pick apart their brains, get them dependent on your rich, fancy Yale degree paid for by your parent's embezzlement and avoidance of tax payments while you were a pampered kid, you cheat on your exam papers and then get people addicted to your... your low-grade clap-trap!'

'Look, Sam, I'm sensing some real conflict here and think it might be best if...'

'You're sensing conflict? Are you Yoda? Do you sense when the dark side of the force moves? Take a look in the mirror, pal, see if you haven't got the glowy evil eyes after all!'

'Sam, I don't believe you're anywhere near the oven or that you're depressed, and I'm afraid I'm going to have to put down this phone now...'

'Hey, doc, doc. Look, it's okay. Sorry I got carried away there. But you gotta realise... you know... I'm not a happy man? God hates me, people blame me for everything that goes wrong, I don't get any credit for all the cool things I do. People take one look at me and go 'aaahhh! The Devil! Run away!' like I'm the big insect thing in that film... oh hell, what's it called? You know, the subways, the big insect thing that ate all the cockroaches and then grew...'

'I'm sorry, I don't watch those kind of films.'

'You don't? Uh.'

'How does that make you feel, Sam? How do you feel about me?'

'I think you're culturally deprived. You ever seen the Mummy?'

'No, I haven't seen the Mummy...'

'It's one of the funniest films on the planet. You've got to see it. Skip the spin-off, though. There's only so much sand a guy can take. There was this great film, though... well, actually, no, that's a lie, it was a crap film really.... but it had the guy from the Godfather...'

'Marlon Brando?'

'No, the younger brother who becomes the Godfather.'

'Al Pacino...'

'Right, him as Satan and he was all cool and swingy and hip and evil in a sharp suit and I thought... I thought, if only I could get away with that look. You know, with the cool kinda twitch of an eyebrow that says, 'I was a mafia boss while you were still watching Popeye' type thing?'

'You're saying you want to be the Devil?'

'Nonononono! I'm saying I want to be Al Pacino being the devil.'

'You want to be an actor?'

'Doc, aren't you listening? I've got the Devil thing all wrapped anyway, it's just the style. I think if I got a make-over people would open up about me, be warmer, associate me with the Godfather and that little theme tune... you know, de-dah-de-dah...'

'Are you saying you believe yourself to be the Devil?'

'Am I allowed yes or no answers?'

'I'm sorry, Sam, but if you really believe this I think I honestly cannot continue this conversation...'

'What's the matter? You're not Catholic!'

'I think that's my business....'

'Come on. Your father's Jewish, your mother's a scientologist. You've been through counselling twice, and I hardly blame you. You embezzle and you cheat and frankly, you're gonna burn in Hell. The question is whether you want the seventh or the sixth circle? I thought we could do a deal... hey, doc?'

'Sam, I'm putting the phone down.'

'It's your funera...'

'You have reached Dr Wendle's office. I'm afraid I'm not in at the moment, but please leave your message after the tone. Thank you.'

'Hey, it's me. Well, obviously it's me. It's Sam. Hey, is anyone there? Is....'

'Hello?'

'Hello. Who's this?'

'I'm... Dr Wendle's secretary...'

'You okay? You sound kinda upset...'

'Are you a patient?'

'Well, kinda, yeah... you okay?'

'I'm... I'm afraid I have some bad news about Dr Wendle. There has been an accident... something fell....'

'It's all going to be fine. Look, sit down, have a tissue, have a cup of coffee. Are you sure you're okay?'

'I'm... just a little shook up. I'll be fine...'

'That's okay. Take a deep breath. What's your name?'

'Scarlet.'

'Tell me, Scarlet, have you ever considered the state of your immortal soul?'

Author profile
Helen Olajumoke Oyeyemi

Helen Olajumoke Oyeyemi was born in Ibadan, Nigeria, on 28 September 1984, but moved to England with her mother in 1988, where her father was studying at Middlesex University.

This was shortly after she'd eaten wet cement and was banned from drinking water for three days, during which she could only drink palm oil.

Helen is currently studying Social and Political Sciences and indulging in Emily Dickinson and Chuck Palahniuk at Corpus Christi College, Cambridge.

Her first novel, 'The Icarus Girl', will be published in January 2005.

ellyday

by Helen Olajumoke Oyeyemi

When Sophie walked into Elly's bedroom, whistling with cold and flexing wind-numbed fingers, Elly jerked as if a whip had just been cracked before her nose. She scrambled up from where she had been reclining on the sofa and flung her arms guiltily around her waist, but Sophie didn't advance on her. Instead, she rammed her hands into the pockets and looked at Elly with eyes calm and flat, as if leaking dead brown light from within.

I know.

'You're - what - I didn't hear you come in,' Elly said, finally.

Her voice was croaky, deep, and full of cogs and edges, as if she had no control over her words and had to stumble haltingly over each one as it came out.

Sophie huffed out a sigh, not looking away from silent Elly, who edged one foot to the other, her fluffy brown hair over one half of her face. Narrowing her eyes, she continued to watch; watching Elly blink drowsily, the prickly

55

downsweep of her eyelashes shading the skin beneath her eyes.

(How to do this. How to talk about this?)

Taking a seat on the end of the sofa, she pointed with unwavering firmness to the spot that Elly had just vacated.

It was Sunday morning, cold, with Christmas four days away, and the open-curtained window sent brittle light careering around the room. The redness of Christmas was somehow in the air, a tingling ribbon of expectancy that made a numb parcel of the minutes and hours.

Expectancy.

Settling herself with one end of Elly's thick grey fleece thrown over her shoulder in a sort of partial toga, Sophie waited for Elly to sit down.

Elly didn't.

Instead, she went to her window sill, to the glinting, silver-mesh box that held her CDs, and started sorting through it. Sophie could see that her hands were shaking.

'I'm putting a CD on - anything you wanna listen to?'

She said 'listen to' like one word, 'lissentooo,' trailing off as if her tongue had just died on her. Sophie impatiently flicked the air with her hand.

'You're not putting a CD on. I'm talking to you."

Elly turned around and leaned against her desk, tugging at her woolly red sleeves with

56

twitching fingers. She regarded Sophie with a slight, nervous smile. 'What?'

Sophie looked at her lap for inspiration; unconsciously jogging her denim-clad legs so that her feet tapped up a feverish pattern on the carpet.

(Oh, how to do this RIGHT?)

'Pull up your jumper,' she said.

'Say what?'

There was steel in Elly now; she was standing straight, and the languor in her voice now sounded like a soft, sibilant hostility. Her shadow was almost straight; it only slanted a little bit, the top of her shadow-head only reaching a few yards away from Sophie's feet. Sophie tried again.

'I just want to see something.'

'See something like what?'

There was no bending in her, only ridged stillness. She had brought the box from her sill to her lap, and was now lifting CDs up, peering at them. It was clear that she couldn't see the covers properly, and was feebly picking out images, registering them slowly. She looked as if her very blood was passing through her sluggishly, crawling with indolence from vessel to vessel and round again.

Oh my God.

'Elly,' Sophie said, as steadily as she could, her

eyes fixed on the row of dancing animals (a hamster with fluffy brown rippling all over it, a rabbit with tall floppy grey ears, a bear wearing a green and black check waistcoat, sitting in a row against the blue-painted wall and staring evenly) on Elly's shelf. She had to remember that she was supposed to be the bossy one, the one who always told Elly what to do, the best friend that Elly's mum didn't really like.

'Elly, please just do it!'

She forced herself to sound irritable, tetchy, as she had so many times before when they were younger, and she'd threatened to stop speaking to Elly if she didn't do what Sophie said.

Elly opened and closed a CD case with a light click. Sophie couldn't make out what the CD was.

'You're only going to get angry,' Elly said, finally.

'I won't, man.'

(Control, control how to DO this right?)

'You will. You always do,' Elly said matter-of-factly, her sentence falling into a drawl again as she pushed clouds of hair behind her ears without looking up.

(Ahlllwaaaaaaysdooo)

Did she have to SPEAK like that?

Sophie lost her struggle and let her voice slip away from her and sound over-loud in the space between them. She couldn't, at that moment, properly care that she was sneering.

'Don't think I don't know that you haven't been EATING!'

(Silence. Elly, having left the CDs alone, now carefully fastening her black velvet jewellery box, which sat on the yellow-painted wood of her desk like a shadow-stain.)

'You think you're clever or something! Baggy clothes, bits of food in tissues... but everyone knows something's wrong with you. You look like some kind of scarecrow or something! Before, you were...'

'Fat,' said Elly, interrupting her with a puzzlingly beatific smile.

Sophie strove to deny what she had been thinking (but not about to say) but Elly spoke vehemently, and the driving, focussed intent in getting her words out clear and rounded, without a slur, was painfully evident.

'I was fat. And you were skinny, and that was okay. But now I'm skinny, you don't like it.'

Sophie gaped, then fell back into the cradling grey material around her feeling strangely as if she needed to hide.

So wrong, this was all so wrong.

Elly sucked her cheeks in, making her face look even more patchily shadowed, and looked at Sophie with sly pity.

'You know it's true,' she added, as if there were

anything more to add.

Sophie stared at the strangeness of her friend, then abruptly stopped jiggling her knees as she realised that her feet had been drumming an irregular rhythm on the floor the whole time.

'You are just full to the brim with crap,' she said, sounding hollow and unconvincing even to herself. 'Just pull up your jumper, you idiot.'

Shaking her head. Elly started to say something, but it was unintelligible, and she broke down and started to cry halfway through.

It was somehow hideous, the crying, as if it were liquid ripped out of her and flooding the room, laboured, gurgling of the horrors inside. Sophie was scared and stayed where she was, her hands frozen in a half-reaching gesture, caught on the silk-fine dividing line between wanting closeness and needing distance.

Elly sank to the floor, holding onto the thick yellow table-leg with both hands, as if it were some talisman that would pull her up and up into the blue... and the weak sunlight.

Pale, pale skin layered on yellow, the hands, gripping, like a ten-fingered bruise. Just as Sophie, tensing to rise, thought that she would fall or faint, or both, Elly gritted her teeth and closed her eyes tight. She stayed, crouching, her shoulders hunched so that she looked neck-less.

Still crouching, she swayed. Her jumper

flapped. God, she was thin. Some part of Sophie separated itself from the nausea of Elly's thinness, the linear slicing of her collarbone, and tried to calculate how much she might weigh, now.

Impossible to tell. She made herself speak, but the kind words, the needed words, had fled away from her in the downward spiral of Elly's falling.

'You can't even talk properly, Elly. You can't even SEE properly. I can't believe you think it's worth it! You need to -'

'You didn't care,' Elly, still choking out sobs, turned her face away and spoke softly, addressing her words to the table-leg.

'You saw it happening. But you didn't care, you didn't say anything. Only when I'm skinnier than you, you care.'

'Elly,' Sophie said, dropping from the sofa to the floor and crawling a little closer, but just out of striking distance. 'Listen: you're not well. You're really ill. It's serious. You need to...you should talk to someone. Yeah? You can't seriously think that I-'

Elly's face was completely hidden by her hair. She kept her head turned away, but she was no longer crying.

She was listening.

Her electric attentiveness broke a gap in the careful, sensible tones that Sophie had been

61

measuring out. She knew she wouldn't be able to make another full sentence without her mouth going dry and her voice faltering, so she simply stopped rather than be heard to fail at speaking.

'Soph.'

Sophie licked her lips.

'Yeah.'

'When is it okay to die?'

'What?'

Alarmed, Sophie rocked back onto her heels.

'What are you talking about?' She gazed around distractedly, trying to gather her thoughts as her vision momentarily closed in on a photograph in the middle of the wall behind Elly's bed. It was a balcony picture - the sky, deep-purple with orange streaks running through it here and there, as if drawn with the end of an idle, trailing finger. Elly always maintained that a picture was spoiled if there were people in it.

'It's nearly Christmas. Soph. When is it okay to die?'

So soft that the words tunnelled into one another and came out in a wisp of almost inaudible breath. No tears in her voice now, but something else.

Sophie stared at the back of Elly's head, and realised, fully realised, that she didn't know this person. The falling away of the flesh and the growing gaunt; all of it was layers unravelled, revealing a secret, knotted heart.

'Are you telling me that you want to die?'

She said it as forcefully as she could, hoping that she had made the idea sound absurd and ridiculous, knowing that she hadn't.

'I asked you a question first,' Elly replied, then frantically hurried her words out before Sophie could say anything else.

'Listen to me, for once, okay? When...is it okay...to die? Like, is it a shame to die before you've ever kissed a boy, or ever been loved, or anything like that? Is it really such a shame, something we should be embarrassed about, as if it's rude to be dead?'

The sense in this, where?

Sophie drew closer to Elly, close enough to touch, and watched the light play on the splitting ends of unbrushed hair standing out all over Elly's head like miniature prickles. She was thankful for the softening of her voice.

'I don't know what you want me to say, Elly - I don't know whether you want me to tell you that it's never okay to die, or -'

Then she stopped speaking and gazed, brimming over, instead.

Elly had pulled up her jumper.

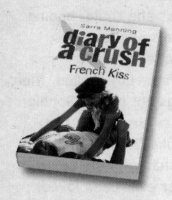

Author profile
Sarra Manning

Sarra Manning is a teen queen extraordinaire, with magazines such as J17 and ElleGirl featuring on her CV. She is now acting editor of 'What To Wear' magazine, as well as writing the 'Shop Bitch' column for Time Out. She's also been a regular contributor to Elle, The Guardian, ES Magazine, Seventeen, Details and Heat.

Her fifth book, 'Pretty Things', is due for publication in 2005 with a sixth book, 'Lost', to follow.

Totally Private
by Sarra Manning

Name:	Edie Wheeler
Age:	Sixteen
Lives:	Manchester via Brighton
Height:	180 cm
Weight:	Sixty-five-Sixty-eight kg (depending on how much ice cream I've eaten in a twenty-four hour period)
Hair:	Getting blonder with every application of Clairol Golden Honey
Eyes:	Blue
Favourite book:	Emma by Jane Austen
Favourite film:	Ghostworld, Bring It On and Breakfast At Tiffany's (it's impossible to pick just one)
Favourite TV show:	Alias (spies kick ass, quite literally)
Lust object:	Jake Gyllenhall, Dean Speed from The Hormones and Dylan
Girl hero:	Drew Barrymore

Favourite website: www.ratemykitten.com
Favourite thing in the world:
My vintage Dior handbag I bought off ebay
Make-up item I couldn't live without:
Lancome Juicy Tubes
Ambition:
For Dylan to fall wildly and passionately in
love with me and take me on a roadtrip
across America

14th September
Do you ever get the feeling that you're waiting
for your life to begin? I feel like I invented that
feeling. Cos today is all about shiny, new things.
Scary, shiny new things. And instead of jumping
out of bed, ready to dazzle the world with my
brightest smile and my cute new hairslides, I'm
huddled under my duvet, scribbling into my Emily
Strange notebook.

   I mean, I guess I should be rising to the
challenge but, y'know not so much. It's my first
day at college so, officially, I'm not a schoolgirl
anymore. And, OK, I might be doing A-levels but
I'm doing 'em at a college where there are art
students and drama students and everyone
(apart from the savage, psycho Barbies studying
Hairdressing who laughed at me in the canteen
on the day I had my interview) is achingly cool.

   So, how come I know that I'm going to feel so

young and phoney compared to everyone else? Like, someone's going to tap me on the shoulder and say, 'Hey kid, you don't belong here, back to school.' But school and my friends are miles and miles away. Why did Dad have to get a new job and decide to transfer me, Mum and Pudding halfway across the country? Because he's hellbent on ruining my life and destroying what little self esteem I have, that's why.

Did my heart love 'til now?

22nd September
I got this massive lecture from the parents at breakfast about 'making more of an effort to fit in' and 'we know the move was hard on you but it's been four weeks and you should have adjusted by now'. I'm sure they've taken lessons in how to make me feel like a socially dysfunctional freak of nature. They don't understand though. All the people in my classes at college were at school/youth club/Brownies together and they just completely ignore me. And, besides, it's really hard to just crowbar myself into someone's conversation, like, 'Me too! I love The Thrills. Isn't the lead singer just the dreamiest?' Insert retching noises. I just can't do stuff like that.

But I knew I wouldn't hear the end of this (my

mother is the missing link between Rottweilers and rat-catchers) so I got pro-active and signed up for a Photography course that starts next week. I might not make any friends but as least I'll learn how to take arty, grainy black 'n' white shots of dead trees and stuff.

So, directly after scribbling my name onto the sign-up sheet on the noticeboard, I was ambling down the corridor, nothing on my mind but whether I should have another packet of Skips, when five minutes later my entire life changed! One moment it sucked and then the next, nothing was going to be the same again. No warning, no stirring music. There I was in the canteen scraping a plastic stirry thing through the hot chocolate granules at the bottom of my cup and hoping no-one would notice me sitting there all alone, when I looked up, locked into a pair of deep blue eyes, and felt my spiritual self shift into orbit.

His face was all hard planes and angles, cheekbones and jawline softened only by these pillowy lips. His hair was equally confused and couldn't decide whether it was a fin or a mullet or just really messy or all of the above. But it was the colour of liquorice, or maybe that really dark chocolate that I can only eat in tiny amounts because it's too rich. He was wearing jeans that were faded on the knees and dark blue everywhere else, a striped shirt and a suit jacket. All of him was in chaos and it was hard to work out whether he was beautifully odd or oddly beautiful. I never knew boys could be beautiful but this one was.

Then he kinda looked beyond me and frowned as if he was annoyed at my audacity for daring to be in his line of vision. Boys that look like that always reckon they can get away with that kind of behaviour. He's probably an arrogant dickweed but what the hell, he's a drop-dead gorgeous, arrogant dickweed.

I saw him again, later that afternoon, striding across the college lawn like the hounds of hell were snapping at his heels. It was like everything around him slowed down and then I heard someone shout, 'Dylan!' and he turned round. His name's Dylan. Of course, he's called Dylan. How could he be called anything else?

25th September
This is what I've found out about Dylan, or the heir to my heart, as I now think of him: He's on the Art Foundation course, and he's 19. He's three years older than me. Age gaps are very sexy. That means he's done his A-levels already. He's one of the in-crowd, along with his two friends, Paul (bleached streaks, old-skool trainers and a Carhatt T-shirt) and Simon (really tall,

69

goatee-d, always wears a black turtle-neck.) They spend a large proportion of each day in the cafe across the road, but upstairs, which apparently is far more socially acceptable than downstairs with all the housewives. Dylan works in Rhythm Records on Wednesday afternoons and all day Saturday.

How do I know all this? Because, I was incredibly brave today and actually spoke to this girl, called Mia, who is on my course.

I was sitting in our English class with an empty desk on the other side of me and an animated, 'I'm just waiting for all fifty of my closest friends to suddenly materialise' expression on my face, when this girl plonked herself down next to me.

I glanced at her but she was rummaging about in her bag so I went back to doodling Dylan's name all over my notebook.

'I like your nail varnish.'

No-one has ever spoken to me at college apart from the teachers, so it took me a moment to process the information that this was actually talking. To me. I looked at a sparkly red nail and then at her. She gave me a look like she thought I was possibly mentally challenged.

'Urn, thanks. I didn't realise you were speaking to me,' I muttered.

She nodded impatiently. 'So, are you from Manchester Girls? I don't recognise you.'

It was strange. Like, she wasn't actually being rude but there was something in her tone of voice that wasn't far off it.

'No, I'm from Brighton,' I said, and I've never been more aware of my posh Southern accent. 'My dad got transferred here over the summer. My name's Edie.'

'Eddie?'

'No, Edie. It's short for Edith,' I mumbled the last bit because I hate the cool trick that my parents decided to put on my birth certificate.

'I'm Mia,' the girl announced. 'I was named after this actress called Mia Farrow.'

'It's a cool name,' I ventured nervously because it was, and after a moment's pause, Mia seemed to let out the breath she'd been holding and smiled at me.

'Thanks. So do you like living here?'

'It's all right,' I said without much conviction. 'I miss my friends though.'

Mia nodded and then glanced over at my notebook, which was lying on the desk with Dylan's name plastered all over it.

'Oh, Dylan,' she grinned knowingly. 'He's very snackable. When did you meet him?'

My face went exactly the same shade as my nail varnish and I stuttered some nonsense about how Dylan was actually the name of a guy from Brighton but Mia wasn't buying it for a second.

'Yeah, right,' she snorted. 'Everyone loves Dylan. It's like a rite of passage thing. You get breasts, you realise that sitting downstairs in Fritzsch's is terminally naff and you fall in love with Dylan.'

'Are you in love with Dylan then?' Just by saying his name, it felt like I'd signed my soul over to the devil.

Mia snorted again. 'No, because I'm in love with his best friend, Paul. He's in love with me too. We're a regular love fest.'

And then she went into this long, complicated story about Paul and his ex-girlfriend that I couldn't really follow but I nodded a lot and then I tried to make a few discreet enquiries about Dylan but I might just as well have had 'I fancy Dylan' tattooed on my forehead. Yeah, that's how subtle I am.

30th September
Dylan sat at the table in front of me today in the canteen, but, like, facing me. I pretended to be engrossed in one of my English books but I couldn't help stealing these glances at him. His left eyebrow is broken by a scar, a thin white line; it made me feel weird every time I looked at it. I wonder how it happened.

I think he was copying someone's homework (do Foundation Art students get homework?)

72

because he sat all hunched over these papers, a pen clenched in his long fingers, and his forehead all crinkled up, like he was deep in thought.

It made me feel sad because even though he was just a couple of metres away from me, he was also a million miles away. He was beautiful and everyone loves him and there I was sharing breathing space with him and he didn't even know I existed.

I felt small and insignificant. He's a proper person. He matters to all sorts of people and I'm just a stupid kid.

And he probably doesn't trip up the bus stairs or lose all his cognitive thought processes when he's in close proximity to someone he fancies. Oh, please don't let him fancy anyone, I thought.

And then he looked up. And his face came to life as this girl sashayed over to him and planted a kiss on his cheek. A pretty, hipster girl with an inky black bob and a slash of crimson lipstick and a cute black mini-dress, which would have looked ridiculous on me.

That would be Shona, Paul's infamous ex-girlfriend. Mia told me all about her yesterday. Apparently her and Dylan have been friends ever since they bonded in a sandpit at nursery school and they practically grew up together. So, that would be good cos they'd be like brother and sister, but I've never seen any siblings lovin' it up

like they were. She was playing with his hair and
HE WAS JUST LETTING HER.

And the other suckiness that was my day? The
people in my English class hate me. They were
sitting on the next table along from me in the
cafe and talking about how I was 'up myself' and
'weird'. Better than being a bunch of cookie-
cutter deadheads.

4th October
I'm just back from a weekend in Brighton,
staying with the grand'rents and hanging out with
my old friends. It's only been a month since I last
saw them but everything seemed different. Toby
and Alice are now going out, which just amazes
me because I can still remember the time we
were rehearsing the Nativity play at infant school
and he wet himself and then pulled baby Jesus'
crib over the puddle. And Alice is snogging him
on a regular basis! Tish has dyed her hair pink.
Eve's parents are splitting up. I can't believe how
much happens in such a short space of time.
They were all talking about the sixth-form college
and having long conversations about people I
didn't know and though they made a big effort to
include me, I felt like I was being left behind. I
know what will happen. The phone calls and the
emails and the monthly visits will all tail off and,
eventually, we'll lose contact. So I won't have any

friends left there and I certainly don't have any friends here.

7th October

I couldn't write last night because my hands were still shaking! Picture the scene: me skulking into that stupid Photography course in combats and a scruffy old black shirt cos I couldn't be arsed to make any effort and then I nearly fall out of my trainers because who's taking up the back row but Dylan! And Paul! And Simon! In fact, the whole class was full of art students (apparently they have to take it as part of their course), so Martyn (the tutor) told me to sit in the back row, next to Paul as there was nowhere else to sit.

It was the most exquisite torture. Paul sort of smiled at me but my face had contorted into this weird grimace. And then Dylan leaned across Paul and spoke to me.

'Hey,' he said in this voice that was all broken glass and silk. 'Have you got a spare pen I can borrow?'

I am the lamest girl in the world. All I could do was shake my head. My tongue had become this heavy, lumpy thing. But when I got my camera out (a 'sorry for ruining your life' present from Dad) I heard him say to Simon, 'She's got a cool camera'!

The photography lesson went straight over my

head. I couldn't take my eyes off Dylan's hands. He's got beautiful fingers; they're really long and thin and look like they should be permanently picking out chords on a shiny, red gee-tar. Also, when the class was over, they all went out for coffee but he held the door open for me and WINKED at me! I can't believe that my stomach lurched at such obvious behaviour but, hey, it did. My everything lurched.

13th October
College has been a lot better. I get on really well with Mia. Well, she goes on and on about Paul (she's made me tell her, like, fifty times about sitting next to him in Photography) and I've started hanging out with these two boys Nat and Trent from my History of Art class. They're really cool. Nat has the naughtiest expression on his face all the time, like he's thinking evil things. And Trent is so pint-sized and cute that I want to pick him up and stash him in my pencil case and take him home. They came over to talk to me when they saw the Pucca sticker on my folder and said that they'd seen me around and had been daring each other to come and say hello. 'Why didn't you just come over and say hi?' I asked them. And Nat just shrugged and said that they were a bit intimidated by me, which is so wrong because I am the least intimidating person

76

in the world. I mean, fluffy little baby bunny rabbits are more intimidating than me.

But the best thing that's happened is that Dylan is now actively aware of my existence! He smiles at me when he sees me. I can't believe I'm being such a wuss over a mere boy-shape, I seem to be losing all my kick-ass faculties. In fact, everything was swimming along quite pleasantly and then life suddenly got seriously heavy and weird. When I got to Photography class yesterday (late as usual, but I had made a special effort and put on my favourite polka dot vintage dress and my new pink Converses), the only seat free was next to Dylan.

I felt as if all the molecules in my body were straining towards him. He was wearing a faded Coca-Cola T-shirt that had these little holes in it, like it was really old. And I realised that if I leaned very slightly to my right, his bare arm would be touching my bare arm, which made me feel almost sick with nerves.

I didn't even dare sneak any sideways looks at him but then Martyn said we had to get into pairs to do this assignment and told us to work with the people next to us. Yup, the impossible just fell right into my lap - Dylan's my photographic partner! But instead of being pleased, it just makes me want to cry.

I couldn't speak at all. He must think that I'm

a complete freak. I had to hide my hands under the table so he wouldn't see them shaking as he tried to talk to me.

'So I guess we haven't been formally introduced,' he said, and he looked at me, and all I could do was stare at my notebook on the table in front of me and know that every part of me was blushing. My face, the tips of my ears, even the bits between my toes. Dylan, to give him credit, soldiered on.

'I'm Dylan, I'm on the Foundation Art course, are you doing A-levels?'

I managed to nod and shrug and shake my head in reply to all his questions. Give it a week or two and I might upgrade to the odd grunting noise.

Dylan had to decide what our project was going to be - which was taking photographs of lots of crumbling buildings, as far as I can tell. He was chattering away about the influence of the Gothic Revival in a lot of Manchester's architecture in the nineteenth century and I could barely hear him, though he did say something about 'flying buttresses' and then laughed.

I think it's fair to say that Dylan's got me down as a mute. Even worse, he's coming here, TO MY HOUSE on Sunday. This is not a good thing, especially as I actually had to talk to him at that point and try to be cool and not forget my address. I started stammering and blushing even more than I already had. It was hideous. And I glanced up and he was just giving me this look accompanied by a little half-smile that just about removed the top layer of my skin.

15th October

I can't concentrate on anything but the fact that Dylan is coming over on Sunday. By some miracle, the 'rents are going to a wedding on Saturday and staying over so they won't be home until very late and my mother won't be barging in, proffering Ribena and oatcakes.

Mia told me that Dylan has a terrible rep and that he's left a 'trail of broken hearts in every girls' school from here to Cheshire.' And that he and Shona have this strange contest to see who can get off with the most people but it's really because they have this love/hate relationship and they're trying to score points off each other. 'Mia, have you seen Dylan?' I asked her incredulously as we sat on the wall by the Nursery Block and split a bag of chips between classes. 'He's gorgeous. If he wanted Shona, he could have her. He doesn't need to play games.'

But Mia just gave me a funny look and then changed the subject.

I can't seem to settle. I wish Sunday was here and then I wish that it was never, ever going to happen. When I'm alone inside my head, I have these amazing conversations with Dylan and I'm funny and intelligent and just a little bit quirky. But in reality I know that I'm just a stupid, dumb girl who's too chicken to even speak to him.

17th October
In twenty-four hours Dylan will be in my house. It's just too awful to contemplate. And if I wasn't stressed enough, Mia's invited herself round to stay over tonight. I like her and all but I just wanted to be alone tonight so I could work myself up into a hysterical state.

18th October
Mia's as good as dead. She came around, spiked my Diet Pepsi with vodka and then persuaded me that it'd be a really good idea to cut a fringe in. 'You've got really cool eyebrows, but no-one can see 'em,' she kept saying. And I felt so woozy that in the end she just kind of lunged at me with the scissors and butchered my hair. Then she threw up on my mum's Art Deco rug.

Dylan's coming round in half an hour (excuse me while I have a mild heart attack). The lounge stinks of Dettol, I've got a killer headache and worst of all, my so-called fringe is crooked and curling up at the ends. I wish I was dead. No I don't - I wish everyone else was dead.

18th October - but later

By the time Dylan actually turned up I was practically hyper-ventilating. Every time I looked in the mirror my fringe had become even more lame. It was flicking out at the edges and just wouldn't lie flat. Did I mention that it was completely uneven too?

I was just in the middle of changing, so I was wearing my knee-length, hipster skirt and the Lisa Simpson T-shirt I'd slept in, when the doorbell rang. I swear to God, my limbs went into spasms. I managed to open the door and Dylan was slouched nonchalantly (my word for the week) against the door jamb, dressed all in black. He slowly uncoiled himself, smiled at me in a not very reassuring way and handed me a carrier bag.

'I thought we could have these with our tea,' he said, with another smile that was a millimetre away from being a smirk.

I just stared at my feet, but eventually I took the bag and looked inside.

He'd brought biscuits. When I glanced at him, he was staring at me really intently. It was my bloody fringe, wasn't it?

You look different,' he said after I'd just stood there and gazed at him for five minutes. Then, he reached out his hand and lifted my chin. My stomach dipped all the way down to the silver nail varnish on my toes. I pulled away cos I just couldn't bear it any longer.

'It's my fringe. I had a run-in with a pair of scissors,' I muttered and he was like, 'Wow, you actually talk!'

And then we were sitting on the stairs and I told him about Mia and he said in this strange, strained voice, 'ah, that sounds like Mia.'

I looked at our knees and mine just looked so small and childish compared to his. Even his knees seem dangerous. Does that sound strange? Anyway, to cut a long story short, quite literally, we ended up in the bathroom so that Dylan could tidy up my fringe. He was really into the idea and I figured that it couldn't look any worse.

He didn't actually seem to be interested in me, but my fringe held a fatal attraction for him.

It was a very, very intimate situation. I sat on the edge of the tub and Dylan knelt in front of me, cupping my chin and turning my head this way and that before he started snipping. I'd always vaguely thought that all boys who cut hair had to be gay - but Dylan seemed so not gay. The way he went about cutting my fringe was more about me being a sculpture or a drawing and him being an artist, moulding clay or smudging charcoal.

And then when he'd finished, he wouldn't let

me look. Instead he did something which freaked me out. He told me to close my eyes and he started, very gently, blowing on my face to get rid of all the icky little hairs. He was holding me by the shoulders to stop me from moving and I wanted him to kiss me so badly. More than I've ever wanted anything.

But he didn't.

He just turned me round to face the mirror and I have to admit my hair was happening. My fringe was really, really short but it suited me. That devastating half-smile which makes me turn into a puddle of not-quite-set jelly was back on Dylan's face again but he just said, 'I've given you Jean Seberg hair. It looks really cute.'

I was sort of 'aw shucks'-ing but he just said dead seriously, 'Your eyebrows are fantastic.' Then the moment was gone, so I went downstairs and made him some tea.

But the kettle had barely boiled before Dylan had to go. It was just, 'Time I wasn't here.' We didn't even take any photos or talk. One moment he was in the kitchen dunking digestives into his tea and I was summoning up the courage to open my mouth and form complete sentences, the next he was out the front door. He didn't even say goodbye. I watched him disappear down the street and as he got further and further away, the sadder I felt. Then I realised the 'rents would be home any minute so I went to inspect the rug for permanent puke damage.

Later on, I googled Jean Seberg. She was a French actress who starred in this film called Breathless (or Au Bout De Souffle) and although she had a crop that I could never get away with, she also had a really short fringe. And was pretty in this really gamine way.

So did Dylan think I was like Jean Seberg; pretty in a gamine way...or was it just my fringe?

I have to stop this obsessing about him but it's almost like I want to consume Dylan whole. When I'm with him, I'm a different person. I become really aware of myself and I'm not sure I like it. I don't know. Why is this whole boy/girl thing so confusing?

19th October

I felt dreadful today like I had this sense of impending doom hanging over me. I spent most of the night thinking about what had happened with Dylan. And I also remembered how unimpressed he was with Mia. I didn't see Dylan at all, but I saw his friend, Paul, who winked at me. Not in a sleazy way, more in a friendly way. I also saw Mia who I thought might apologise for puking on my mum's rug. But she just sneered at me and said, 'Your fringe is ridiculously short.' And I said, 'Well, whose fault is that?' Then she muttered something under her breath about girls with stupid crushes and how I should just get a life. So, then I was like, 'Oh yeah, I had a great time with Dylan on Sunday in case you were interested and Paul's just winked at me.' She kind of shoved me against the wall and then stormed off.

Nat and Trent said that I looked like a young Angelina Jolie and when I beamed at them, they nudged each other and laughed and I was like,

'Yup, that was the right thing to say.'

Author profile
Serena Mackesy

Serena Mackesy is a novelist, journalist and travel writer. Her novels, 'Virtue' and the bestselling 'The Temp', were both published to great critical acclaim. Her third novel, 'Simply Heaven', a comic-gothic yarn of class clash and murderous in-laws, will be published in January 2005. She lives in London.

The Kiss
by Serena Mackesy

He doesn't comment on the beds. Time was, he
would have taken the sight of two single beds
fixed to the wall as a challenge, would have
thought the prospect of six nights beyond arm's
reach justification for unpacking the Swiss Army
knife and hunkering down to find a solution. But
now he merely drops his shoulder-bag on the
nearest and stalks in silence to contemplate the
view from the terrassa.

He doesn't speak. Hasn't since they joined the
queue for check-in. Conrad is a bad traveller;
hates the queues and the waits and the random
seating; hates, most of all, the slap-in-the-face
reminders that, despite the toil, the ambition, the
explosions of late-night hubris, he is, in his late
thirties, the sort of person who buys his holidays
by the package. That no-expense-spared is one
of those phrases that has only ever applied to his
honeymoon. That he is, in effect, no different
from the people whose elbows he squirmed away
from in the sticky confines of Air 2000.

Maggie hauls her own bag in from the tiny

living-room-cum-kitchenette and feels her heart sink. His stance is eloquent as he stares at the building site on the far side of the storm drain. Look where you've brought me, he says, wordlessly. It's all your fault. Your fault. He unfolds his arms, sighs, opens the sliding door and steps outside.

Maggie puts her bag on the stand, stands back and presses her palms into the small of her back. Looks around the apartment – white walls, stained wood units, marble-effect tiles in dust-mask grey, two solid electric rings and an extractor hood, pine sofa-bed, matching armchair and coffee table, nebulous flower upholstery by Giorgios of Agora – in the hope of finding some detail to be positive about. There is little of note. Nothing attractive, but nothing so grisly it could form the basis of a shared joke, furnish them with blitz-spirit anecdotes to prove their unity with. It is simply an outpost of the International Republic of ApartHotel: tarnished grout, limescale-clogged detachable shower hose, two steel-framed prints of local seascapes. They could be anywhere. As it is, they are in Tenerife.

She follows him onto the balcony, feels the internal lurch again as she sees the view. A storm drain. A couple of villas. A dusty road and, thirty metres away, the levelled-out wasteland of an abandoned building site. At least, she hopes it is abandoned. It being Sunday, she has no way of being certain. The shoreline is scattered with majestic, rusted cranes, but the brochure claimed that they were coming to a little-known backwater, an idyllic fishing village, a peaceful beauty spot a short taxi ride from the bright lights of Playa de las Americas.

There are two palm trees. They appear recently to have had a thorough pruning.

'It's not so bad,' she says, hopefully.

There was a time when it wouldn't have been, when they could have wrung enjoyment from the ramshackle nature of their accommodation. They would have hired a car, explored, spent lazy lunchtimes eating olives and manchego in a roadside bodega, kept the curtains closed and used the opportunity for leisurely lovemaking. Love makes you unconcerned about your surroundings. They become all-important when the unconcern is in the heart.

She is tired. Tired of trying, tired of plastering on a smile and cluck-cluck-clucking her way through the day, tired of being held responsible for his unhappiness, his disappointment. Sometimes she wants to scream at the sky, flail at him with her fists, but of course she doesn't. As she watches him, drinks in the downturned mouth, the reproachful shoulders, the tension in the hand that grips the railing, she feels an urge to slap him, to shout: it was you who insisted you needed a holiday. It was you who set the budget, chose the dates, refused to compromise, refused to involve yourself in the choices. What did you want? A miracle?

Conrad heaves a sigh. 'Right, well,' he says, and goes inside.

If you live in the nicer parts of the capital, rarely go where the poor people are, you are shielded, most of the time, from the reality of the obesity epidemic. It's only when you go to the provinces, or on holiday where your fellow countrymen go, that it hits you in the face. The Las Sirenas Apartments (named, apparently, after the mermaids who inhabit a local bay; she enjoys the idea of such mythical company; he, in his uncooperative mood, despises the residents for their superstitious natures) are awash with untrammelled flesh. Mottled, dimpled, crystalline, pendulous: curtains of flesh enveloping the backs of bikini tops, satchels of fat leaving great white stripes across the upper reaches of scarlet thighs, people hobbling like foot-bound Chinese aristocrats from sunlounger to edge of pool, glimpses of hardened skin where relentless friction has formed a carapace.

Maggie knows she shouldn't indulge in the sneering habit, knows that it's far more complicated than that, that these enfolding layers are as likely a product of unhappiness, of emptiness, poverty and tiredness as they are simple greed. But she's not a saint, can no more control the surges of gleeful contempt than she could control the urge to eat chocolate. How can they let themselves get like that? She thinks. What lack of self-respect...? The complex smells of beer and cooking oil; it hangs over the pool like a cloud as the all-inclusive guests mournfully sedate themselves with egg and chips, burger and chips, saveloy and chips. Last night she and Conrad walked down to the harbour and silently ate lobster washed down with a bottle of rose. She caught sight, momentarily, in a reflection in a window as a car passed behind them, of herself and her husband: she huge-eyed with the desperation of a failing marriage, he staring dismally out at the lights of the harbour. My God, she thought, we've become one of those couples we used to laugh at. Eating in silence because the words have run out.

The shock is so great that she orders crème brulee, eats it in seconds as he drums his fingers on the table impatiently, his eyes narrow with unspoken judgements.

Maggie has put on a bit of weight herself lately; is having to accept that it's not all about stingy cutting on the part of the designers. She tells herself it's the onset of middle age, but she's only 35.

He refuses to sit by the pool, saying it depresses him; takes to lying on his bed all day, dozing and reading books from the paperback selection in the ice-cream shop: John Grisham, Clive Cussler, a Virginia Andrews that has been sitting on the stand for so long that the pages have turned yellow. At least come outside, she says. The sun will make you feel better. He refuses, sharply. He doesn't want to be out there among those...

'Well, why don't we go on a trip, then?' she asks. Hears the edge of plaintiveness in her voice and derides herself for it. 'Hire a car? Walk down and sit on those rocks on the edge of the harbour, go swimming?'

He sits up, slams his book face-down on the bedcover. 'Look,' he says, 'I'm tired, okay? Is that too hard to get through your head?'

Maggie shrugs. Picks up her sarong and goes to lie by the pool. Hides her tears behind a pair of sunspecs.

So this is what despair feels like, she thinks. To be trapped by timidity in an existence which barely merits the label life. She knows it's fear which keeps her here: fear of coping, fear of loneliness, fear of the unknown. They have been

together for most of her adult life and she barely
remembers how it was to be without him. And if
she finds it so hard to live with the gnawing,
aching emptiness that assails her now, in
company, how would she survive in solitude?
Meals for one and the tick-tick-tick of the clock?

You couldn't be more alone than you are right
now, says the small voice. Can there be a greater
loneliness than this, than scrabbling after crumbs
of approval, thirsting for affection in an arid
landscape?

She can see mountains. Beyond the villas,
beyond aparthotels, beyond the cranes, they
rear up bare and distant and self-possessed.
She longs for them. Longs for difference. Lacks
the courage to drive alone on unfamiliar roads,
lacks the desire, now, to ask for his company.
He has found a copy of The Spectator in his
suitcase, sits on the balcony poring over it,
little snorts of recognition escaping through
his nostrils. The sight of him in his chino shorts
and his seersucker shortsleeve, pleasuring
himself with the illusion of his unashamed elitism,
scratching behind his ear and pointedly ignoring
her, triggers a surge of rage deep in her stomach.
The urge to throw something, to grab a heavy
ceramic ashtray and slam it down on his thinning
pate is so strong that she has to grip the frame

of the sliding door with both hands to stop herself acting on it.

'Huunh," chortles Conrad. Pinches his nose and smirks.

They always say that holidays bring out the worst in troubled relationships. She had set out hoping that the R&R might revive moribund eroticism, restore, even if only briefly, the old connection. That it might give her something to hope for. But now, the sight of him, his pinky lodged firmly in his right ear, delving, makes her skin crawl.

'Come for a walk," she says on the fifth day.

She has been bargaining with God. Give me some sign, she has said; anything, however small. Show me that there is some willingness left, that we aren't doomed to spend the rest of our lives in this cycle of nag and rebuff, nag and rebuff. I promise I won't nag him any more. I promise: I'll ask once and then I'll leave it. He pushes me into justifications, repetitions, and then they make him angry. I will stop, I swear, if only you will make him listen.

'No, ta,' he says.

She stands rigid, digs her nails into her palms with the effort of saying nothing.

He glances over the top of his paperback. 'Oh, for God's sake,' he says, 'stop bloody nagging for one minute, will you?'

And now she strides through scorching, silent
siesta, barely aware of where she is going,
risking a twisted ankle with her furious tears,
hearing nothing but the howl of her internal
voice. You have deserted me, she blames the
unresponsive God. I asked for your help and you
left me. All I need is a sign, something to tell me
that it will not always be like this...I cannot go on,
God, I can't go on. This life is no life. I need a
sign...

The metalling on the road gives way to a dusty,
rising, eroded track. It is four in the afternoon
and the restaurants are closed, locals asleep in
the breeze from table-fans, tourists locked inside
their complexes, spilling over their sunloungers
and frying in corn oil. Her underused muscles,
burning, slow her down, but she pushes ahead in
her beaded wedges, sweat tickling the turn of her
cheek, soaking her cleavage, slathering her
thighs. How did I get like this? What happened to
me? I used to...

A clamber past sandstone boulders, and the
track ends at a broad plateau strewn with rocks
and spiky succulent shrubs. She stops to breathe
when she reaches the level, hands pressed into
the small of her back. The air is rich with the
scent of thyme and baked earth and oleander.

The mountains, shrouded in heat haze, look like a painted backdrop against the sky. She walks on, drawn by the whiz of ozone and the thunder of waves on the far cliff-face.

Beauty has a wild capacity to leave its observers desolate. She reaches the rocks at the cliff-edge and the view rips her heart from her chest, wrings it out. The fierce Atlantic has worn a horseshoe gouge in the shoreline: rock overhangs a vertiginous plummet into boiling sea. To her right, a small shingle beach, empty, a goat-track zig-zagging down the face of the landward precipice.

Now this is scenery, she thinks. This is why people travel.

She steps forward to see. Forgets, until it is too late, that if there is an overhang on all the other sides, there will be one beneath her as well.

The ground slips away beneath her.

Maggie, panicking, throws herself backward. Snatches at air, feels her palms connect with hot friable rock. Hangs a moment, drinking in the thorn-thick plain in front of her, freezing cold, legs hanging useless, and bargains once again with the Almighty. Save me. Please save me. Make me live through this and I will never succumb to self-pity again. I'll leave him, if that's what you want. Or I'll stay. Just let me live...

And God makes the stone turn to dust beneath

her hands. Makes it slippery as satin. She spirals down toward the angry sea.

A second's elation as she hits the water, plunges downward without encountering an obstruction. My God, I lived! I didn't die! But as she kicks for the surface, feels the undertow suck, suck, suck and pull her away from the light, hope collapses. He didn't want you to go quickly. He didn't want to make it merciful. He wants you to experience each salty moment of your death...

And now she tumbles over and over in the current, catching clothes, limbs, hair, skin on jagged surfaces. Salt stings her eyes and soon, she knows, it will sting her lungs, rack her with a pain that will only ease with unconsciousness. And as she struggles, all she can think is: Conrad. I'm sorry. I'm so sorry. I see it now. Not all the fault was on your side. And you will never know. You will never know how much I loved you, to the end. Oh, Conrad, please know I loved you.

Her body gives up the struggle. Her mouth, against her will, opens, lets out the last of air, breathes in.

And then there are hands. Strong, gentle, calming hands stroking the hair from her face, hooking themselves beneath her armpits, another pair of arms wrapping themselves about her waist. Her eyes, open, see something she knows is impossible: two beautiful, naked women, serene smiles and dancing eyes, floating hair and full-moon breasts and long silver tails like fishes. They look into her face, and their expression is loving, Madonna-like. So this is how it feels to die, she thinks. There is mercy here after all. And she gives herself up to them, relaxes into their protective clasp.

The tails, smooth, shiny, muscular, kick, and the three of them shoot upwards, backward, away from the rockface, out of the grip of the current. Maggie, unbelieving, lets it happen, accepts this strangeness like a newborn infant. They break surface. Air and sunlight. Precious use to one whose lungs are full of water. They are holding her up, now, as they race toward the beach. She feels them slice the water, sees the clouds race past and begins to black out.

She is woken by a blow to her back. Violent, agonising, but very real. Another. And a third. She has never felt strength like it. It is like being hit with a wrecking ball. Water and phlegm explode from her body, gout across the surface of the sea. She hears a whooping noise, feels air go in, coughs, throws up, breathes while they hold her in cradling arms. This is a dream, she thinks. This cannot be real. In a moment I shall wake and…

Shingle beneath her feet. They have brought her to shore. Maggie has never felt more grateful for anything in her life than she is to feel these stones. The hands loosen, adjust, and with a heave she is knee-deep, stumbling, crawling back onto the blessed dry.

She drags herself a few feet from the waterline, collapses onto her side, heaving, weeping. She is wrung out, enervated. Her limbs are made of lead. And she is alive.

The sun goes down soon after six o'clock this close to the equator: long enough that her clothes are nearly dry. Walking barefoot through the town, she glances down the alleyway to the harbour and sees him, pale in the gloom, his hand on his hips, looking out to sea. She walks down the steps to meet him, smiles as he feels her approach, turns and runs toward her.

'Where have you been? Where have you been?'

'I went for a walk,' she tells him.

'But you were gone so long. I thought something had happened. I thought I'd… I'd…'

Standing on the step above him, she reaches out, pulls him toward her, holds his head against her shoulder.

'You don't need to worry about me,' she says. 'I'm sorry if I scared you.'

'I wouldn't know what to do,' he says. 'I wouldn't know what to do if…'

She takes his hand. Kisses the knuckles and

presses them to her cheek. 'It's okay,' she says. 'Come on. I'll take you home.'

Author profile
Julia Green

Julia Green has always loved to write – as a child she kept notebooks and wrote everywhere, especially on train journeys.

Her favourite books are 'Tom's Midnight Garden', 'The Children of Green Knowe', all the stories of Laura Ingalls Wilder – and later, 'Wuthering Heights', 'Jane Eyre' and 'Middlemarch'.

'My stories were often echoes of things I'd read. I used to wish we lived somewhere remote and wild, like Laura Ingalls Wilder, or that I could travel back in time.'

'Baby Blue' was published in April 2004.

Will's Story
by Julia Green

I'm waiting for Mia in the beach café. I'm the
only customer, even though it's lunch time. It's
the end of the season. End of the summer. Mill
Cove campsite will be closing this weekend.
That's where I've been working since June, just
up the road from here.

Mia's been up a few times, for the day. She
gets the bus from Whitecross. Her, and him. I
hardly ever get to see her by herself any more.
I'm not allowed to complain, of course. Not after
what she's been through. I've had it easy, she
says. I haven't a clue. I suppose she's right. But
it's not easy for me, either. It's turned my life
upside down too.

There's this moment, each time, when I see
her getting off the bus up at the main road, that
still makes my stomach flip, even after
everything that's happened. Her pale face, heart-
shaped, and her dark hair that's all feathery and
soft now she's growing it again. She'll be wearing
jeans, and maybe that short stripy top, and she'll
have a huge bag of stuff, since she's going to

spend the night. But it's not like you think – not like that at all – cos he'll be there too. Kai.

I've got to get my head round it. 'You've got to make up your mind, Will,' Mia said on the phone last week. 'Are you going to be involved, or not?'

Am I?

Rachel's making her way over to my table. She's one of the girls who works here. She's gorgeous, and she knows it. You can see her looking at her reflection in the big glass window when she goes past with a tray of drinks or sandwiches or whatever. Ben fancies her. Ben's my brother. Pain in the backside but he's got his uses. Like, he has a car. He's going to teach me to drive (just over two months, now, to my 17th).

'Want anything, Will?' Rachel says.

'Nah. Thanks. Waiting for the bus.'

She goes and stands at the window. Every so often she glances at me. I smile back at her. Well, why not?

It's been a good laugh, working at the campsite all summer. Hanging out at the beach, the café. Being away from home and all the hassle. But this is the last week I've got the caravan. The other summer workers have already left, so I've got it to myself. Which is why Mia can stay over. And Kai, of course.

The sun seems thinner, now it's September.

Even the beach is different. The shadows are longer. The swallows have gone. The café will be closing up too.

Here comes Zoe. She's just a little kid, about three.

'Make me a nanimal, Willum,' Zoe says.

I sometimes make these animals for her out of the paper napkins: I can do frogs, and birds. Zoe's always running about in here, getting under everyone's feet. At first I thought she was Rachel's little sister - Rachel's mum owns the café - but it turns out she's Rachel's sister's kid. They all look after her, the whole family, and the other girls who worked over the summer, and Zoe calls them all mum. I guess she's kind of mixed up.

'There you go, Zoe.' I hand her the paper-napkin frog. We make it hop around the table. Then Zoe wanders off again, sucking her thumb.

I can hear the bus now, grinding up the hill. In a while it will screech down this side as if it's not going to brake in time, as if it'll keep on going straight on to the beach and into the sea.

I can see the sea from where I'm sitting. It's high tide. A pale grey-blue, lapping on to white sand. It looks like something off the telly: an island paradise, except once you get out there you feel how cold the wind is and there's a stinky seaweed smell from where it all got washed up in the storm last week.

School starts next week. It seems so long since we were there I can hardly imagine what it'll be like, sitting in those dusty classrooms. After the exams I never wanted to open a book again, but that feeling's changed now too. I've had enough of mopping floors and cleaning wash basins and toilets and emptying bins and all that crap. Imagine doing a job like that for ever.

It won't be the same, A Levels. Won't be the same crowd. Becky's going to college to do hers, and Liam's moved to Cardiff. Mia won't be there, of course, but then she hasn't been all year.

The bus is stopping. There she is.

She hasn't seen me yet. It gives me one last moment to get ready. To see her with him. To work out what I'm going to do.

She looks amazing. Jeans: yes; stripy top: no. Denim jacket. Frowning. Looking around.

There he is, too. Kai. A small bundle dressed in blue. It's still a shock, every time. Can't get the hang of it. First time I saw him, I thought I'd die.

I was still furious with Mia. For having him. For doing it anyway, whatever I wanted or didn't want. When she so easily could've NOT had him.

After Becky came and told me Mia'd had the baby, I spent all night out on the beach, just walking, mostly, trying to get something – anything - clear in my head, until it was dawn and I was freezing cold and then I just found myself walking to the hospital at Ashton, on auto pilot. I hadn't a clue what I was going to say.

I got to the ward without anyone seeing, and found her single room, easy as anything, as if it was all meant to be. And there he was. In her arms. This tiny baby, with her dark hair. But he didn't have her dark brown eyes. His were blue. Like mine. It did me in completely.

Me. Will. Sixteen years old.

These tears just came in my eyes without my being able to stop them. Mia looked – well – we weren't going out together by then, of course, but she looked wrecked, and washed out, but also older, as if she'd grown up or something. She held the baby like she knew just what to do.

And I just legged it.

Before, I couldn't get it into my head that this baby was actually going to be real. All the stuff that Mum tried to get me to talk about, well I just couldn't. Eventually Mum started saying things like, at least get your exams, and sort yourself out. No point in wrecking yet another life. They've been pretty good about it, really, I suppose. After they got over the shock to begin with, that is. And I did OK in the exams, in spite of everything. Dad doesn't say much, but I kind of know he was pleased.

Mum gives Mia money. She's stopped trying to give her advice. About her *education*, college, nurseries: things like that. Mia wasn't having any of it.

She's stubborn, Mia. You can't tell her anything. She's not like anyone else I know.

We weren't going out or anything, but I didn't stop thinking about her. And then I started seeing her around again, with the baby. There was this day, just after the last exam, on the scraggy pebble beach at Whitecross, very early morning. She was sitting there with the baby, in the place where we'd all had a party the night before – not Mia, of course – and I made up the fire again, and we chatted, and then later she came to Mill Cove with me for my interview for this job, and so it all started up again. Her and me. Except that everything's different. We haven't slept together. Not again. Not yet...

About a week ago, when I went home to Whitecross to see everyone, Mum got out these old photographs of me when I was little. She left the album lying about. She knew I'd look at them. I did. I stared at those baby pictures and I didn't feel a thing. Couldn't connect them with me. It was just some baby in all those photographs. All except one. There was just one that felt different. I kept going back to it. In the end, I nicked it out of the album and stuck it in my pocket. Don't know why. I brought it back with me. I keep looking at it.

In it, my dad's holding me, a small baby in one of those zip-up babygro things. He's holding me round my middle with his big hands, as if I'm flying through the air towards him, head height. And he's looking at me as if he's never seen anyone so cool and wonderful in his whole life before. He's got this huge grin on his face, ear to ear. Hard to imagine, me that size. Dad looking like that. Still, there's the proof. Dad has his lips all pursed up, ready to kiss that little wonderful baby.

And that's me. Me, with my dad.

Get that in your head, Will.

Mia's seen me now. She's waving, and she's dumped the bag down on the path while she gets Kai sorted. She's unbuckling the buggy straps to get him out. He likes to be carried. He's four months old now. He's changing all the time. He'll be sitting up by himself soon, Mia says, and then he'll crawl and be walking and talking...he'll be like Zoe, the kid in the café, into everything and asking questions and just taking it for granted that you want to talk back.

That's Kai, and I'm his dad.

His dad.

The only one he's got.

Rachel's sitting at the window, still watching me. She's got a sort of faraway, sad look on her face. Zoe is climbing onto her lap. It's gone quiet in the kitchen, out the back. It's like everything's stopped still.

This is it. This is when I finally have to make up my mind. Stop pretending he's nothing to do with me. Start realising I might, just possibly, make a difference. To Kai.

So.

I know what I'm going to do.

I'm going to go down to meet Mia, and I'm going to hold out my arms for Kai and I'm going to fly him in for a kiss.

Author profile
Melissa Nathan

Melissa Nathan was born and raised in Hertfordshire and now lives in North London with her family. She was a journalist for ten years before she started writing novels full time. She is the author of 'Pride, Prejudice and Jasmin Field', 'Persuading Annie' and 'The Nanny'.

Her fourth book 'The Waitress' was published in August 2004.

The Journey
by Melissa Nathan

With thanks to Dorothy Parker

Oh, I'd love a lift, thanks!

No thanks, I'd rather walk. I'd rather walk half an hour in the rain without an umbrella than have to pretend to be grateful to sit next to you and make crappy conversation while you 'take' me home. I don't need to be 'taken' anywhere. I'm a big girl now thanks. And what car is it? I bet it's a red sports car with lots of litres in its engine. I bet you wouldn't have offered if it was a purple Nissan Micra.

I like walking. I honestly like walking. I like not getting polluted and I like the exercise. Each leg, like a powerful piston, working my strong body in the direction I choose. Freedom, direction, purpose.

So why couldn't I say no?

Hmm. Because people were watching and I'm a polite girl and I didn't want to humiliate you with honesty. And anyway, no one believes the truth – that I choose not to have a car or a man; that I prefer to be in control even if that means half the population pity me and the other half ignore me.

I choose not to be one of those legless women you see in passenger seats of every car on the road, being driven by someone else in a car they didn't choose, when everyone knows they can drive quite well themselves and walk even better.

Of course I can wait! I'm just grateful for the lift.
   And so it starts. I relinquished control the second I said yes. I'm just the passenger now, a disenfranchised hanger-on. You chat to someone loudly about nothing, safe in the knowledge that you have a status symbol, a female for your passenger seat. I could have been half-way home by now – and smelt the conifers on the corner of Wellbourne Street as I passed them. I could have walked past a stranger and locked eyes for a single light moment of mute understanding. I could have grown a thought and travelled somewhere new. I could have glimpsed someone's warmly lit living room and snatched a slice of their intimate world. I could have hummed a bit and listened to how my voice fills my head. I could have got home all warm and rosy, all satisfied and fresh.

No I'm fine really. Please don't feel rushed just because of me. Yes that's right, Brecknell Avenue, Number 21a. It's only a five-minute drive from here, but of course it takes longer to walk.

So now you know where I live. Don't think you're getting asked in mate. Oh no. Those might be your rules but they aren't mine. I don't owe you anything. Why on earth should I let you into my sacred territory just because you've driven one minute out of your way home? Oh good God, you're getting your keys out already. We haven't even left the church hall and the keys are out. Jingle jangle, jingle jangle.

Ooh, is that a camera? Or a keyring? Oh you are kidding!

It's both. Yes, I'm bowled over by your ability to buy stuff. It's going to be a bloody sports car isn't it?

Ooh, what a lovely car! And red! How stylish! I'll feel like a Bond girl!

Does that mean I die in the first scene? If you drive like Bond, I'm getting out. I don't care if it kills me. Mind you, if you drive like Bond, staying in would probably kill me too. Oh great. CDs all over my seat. No, I don't care what they are. I don't give a flying fart what music you listen to.

Ooh Celine!

I may just barf. If you drive like a tosser while listening to her, I may actually be physically sick.

Ooh, you do drive fast don't you? Even over road humps. It's like Alton Towers!

I'm sick there too. I knew it. You think you're Bond. I'd get out, but you've centrally locked me in. Do you honestly think that in a world full of torment and cruelty, a world that's a spiralling vacuum of meaningless pain followed by infinite nothingness, that I'd be impressed by central locking?

Fifty feet? That's amazing! And I see what you mean, people really do stare don't they?

They're laughing.

I feel famous.

Like Princess Di – really happy. My, what a journey of discovery this is turning out to be. I never knew it was a sign of virility to only use two fingers on a steering wheel and push your foot down on a pedal.

I think we just killed a cat.

Oh bliss. Nearly home and not dead. Perhaps that was my discovery – to come to realise that I do want to live.

Well here we are! Yes, that was quick! Yes, just down here and stop by that lamppost.

Then drive home.

Thank you so much, I really appreciate it. I know, I really should get a car, but I'm useless with machines. I don't like things I can't talk to. I know! Stupid really.

No, don't put your arm round the back of my seat. Just because it's your car, it's still my seat. And you don't have to get close to show me how nice your eyes are. I'm discerning, I'm not blind. And I'm not going to ask you in.

Well I'm sure you must need to get back.

Go away.

No? Morning off? Lucky you. How did you manage that?

Oh Jesus Christ. You're going to tell me.

Look this is silly. Why don't you come in for a coffee?

Right mate. My turn. Travis it is. If I'm going to be bored to death, it might as well be in the comfort of my own home.

Here we are. Just get my keys out. I know. The light's broken. I must get it fixed.

Don't stand so near – as if you're protecting me from my own doorstep. I've stood on this doorstep many times and I've never felt

vulnerable so don't try and make me feel it now.
I know all my neighbours, I bet you don't know
yours.

Yes that's right. Mainly Asian families.
   I can hear your brain working, you don't need
to sigh.

*I know it's a run-down area, but you get so much
more for your money here.*
   How long does it take to make one coffee?
You'll be out in half an hour tops, quicker if Sylvia
does her fur-ball trick. And then I can relax. It'll
all be over. Next week I'll get a travel pass, so
I've got an excuse. Ah! The freedom of planning
ahead! Don't mind my suddenly smiling at you
like that – but I feel overcome with a sense of
soaring, untouchable escape.

*Every week? You're sure? Both ways? Oh! Oh,
how... I don't know what to say.*
   No?

*Yes you're right. Thank you. I'll just say thank
you.*

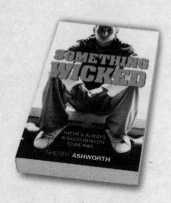

Author profile
Sherry Ashworth

Sherry Ashworth was born in 1953 and grew up in London. Literature, Sherry says, is her passion...both reading and writing.

Sherry started writing for publication in 1989. She has now written a total of eight adult novels and three for young adults, including 'What's Your Problem', which was longlisted for 'Children's Book of the Year Award' in 1999. All of her books are set partly or wholly in Manchester, because, as she says, 'of its vibrant working-class culture, its varied ethnic communities, and also because I know it so well'.

'Something Wicked' was published in June 2004.

The Scream
by Sherry Ashworth

So there I am, in the back room of the salon, just starting on my second coffee of the day, when –

'Linda!'

I freeze, the coffee half-way to my lips.

'Linda! It's your two o'clock.'

I check my watch. It's ten to two. Great. Don't you just hate people who are ultra efficient and have to be ten minutes early for everything? Since half nine this morning I'd not stopped. I'd been cleaning basins, getting all that hairy gunge out of the plugholes, sweeping the floor, washing mugs, making coffee, breaking off at eleven to help Coral with a colour, at 11.30 I had a cut and blow dry, then a perm – being junior stylist at the OK Coral Salon sucks.

My coffee's too hot to drink, so instead I grab a chocolate biscuit and wolf it down – that's today's diet down the drain. For the fiftieth time that day I wonder what I'm doing here – me, Lisa Denton – who was going to be a TV celebrity, or a director of a international company, or the author of a best-selling book. Yeah, right.

I brush the crumbs off my black top and curse as some of them wedge themselves down my bra. I rush out to the front of the salon and go up to the desk where Camilla is taking down the details of an appointment, the phone jammed between her shoulder and her ear. There's only four full-timers at the salon – Coral, the owner, Camilla, her daughter – receptionist and professional layabout – Marsha, Senior Stylist, and me. I'd been just the junior until I finished my course at college – now I'm Junior Stylist – still the lowest of the food chain. This week Marsha's off in Tenerife with her boyfriend and so Coral was kindly letting me help out her appointments. Big privilege, so no extra cash.

Camilla puts down the phone and gestures with an immaculately polished nail to a lady sitting on the black leather settee by the window. She's leafing disdainfully through Hello! Magazine, then checking her watch. As I approach her, she looks up. Immediately I think I know you from somewhere. But there's not time to think where.

She looks me up and down, frowning.

'I was expecting Marsha.'

'She's ill,' I say. 'We thought you wouldn't want to miss your appointment, so I'm doing you.'

It's a lie, but I was told to say that so none of the punters would cancel. Meanwhile, this woman and I continue to stare each other out, like two boxers in a ring. She's trying to decide whether to go ahead with the appointment; I'm frantically trying to work out where I know her from. Perhaps I'd just seen her before in the salon, but I don't think so. And why does she make me feel uneasy – scared, even? Me, lippy Linda, who can give as good as she gets?

'Well, since you've not given me any notice, and I have an important occasion this evening, I suppose I have no choice,' she snaps. 'But I'd like to complain to the manager.' We look around for Coral but naturally she'd done a runner.

I place one of our plastic capes around the woman's shoulders and lead her to the chair where I work. She sits down and stares at herself in the mirror. I stare at her too. Short dark-haired, looks in her fifties or sixties. Trace of red lipstick on her lips. Pinched nose, broken veins on her cheeks. Small, dark, beady eyes. They trouble me, and for a split-second I want to be anywhere else but here. Instead I ask:

'What can I do for you?'

Now she smiles, only that doesn't soften her face. Now she reminds me crazily of the wicked Queen from Disney's Snow White. She leers into the mirror.

'I was thinking of a restyle – to get away from this pudding basin look,' she simpers. 'Something a little bit younger-looking.'

Younger-looking. I'm running through in my head the cuts I can do when Coral calls over.

'Linda! You've left the tap running!'

The tap running. I hate that expression because...because...I look at the woman. I cannot believe my eyes. I know exactly who she is. Miss Hartner - head of my old Primary school and my teacher in Year Five.

There I was, standing sobbing in front of the class, and she's saying to everyone. 'Look at Linda – she can't turn her taps off. Turn your taps off, Linda!'

I was crying because I hadn't been able to do my sums. I couldn't work out what to do with the numbers that you were supposed to carry over. She'd hauled me out to the front of the class and shown everyone my messy answer book. They'd all laughed dutifully. I'd started to cry.

'Well?' asked Miss Hartner. 'Off on holiday, are you?' Another of her odd expressions. She meant, was I daydreaming? I summoned myself back to the present. She's asked me for something younger-looking.

'Something younger,' I repeated. 'Yes – what about – a sort of elfin look – with feathery bits – framing your face – to soften it,' I mumbled. She seems quite content.

'Ye-es,' she says. 'That might work very well.'

I take her over to the basin and begin the shampoo.

'Too hot for you?' I ask.

'No,' she said, her horrid little face spread out backward below me.

I wondered why she hadn't recognised me and then thought it hardly surprising. I wasn't that mousy kid who wouldn't say boo to a goose, who came weeping into school every morning because she was so frightened of getting shouted at and ridiculed. Who was too scared to tell her mum that a teacher had it in for her because she thought she'd never believe it.

As soon as my mum would let me, I had my hair dyed blonde, then my nose pierced. I quite like the goth look, so I wear heavy eye-make up, liner, thick mascara. I carry on shampooing, hardly believing whose hair I'm handling.

'Conditioner?' I ask.

'No,' she says, 'My hair's in naturally good condition.'

'Yes,' I tell her, thinking otherwise.

I towel her head up and lead her back to the chair. She smiles, preens herself, obviously thinking she's the cat whiskers.

'I need to look rather special tonight,' she pouts into the glass.

'Hot date?' I ask, instantly regretting my irony.

125

She fails to notice it. 'No, it's a dinner. A retirement dinner.' She pauses. 'Mine.'

Obviously I'm supposed to be amazed that someone as youthful as her would be retiring. But I won't take the bait. Instead I question her carefully.

'Where from?'

'The school I'm headmistress at. The staff are taking me to dinner at Bella Pizza. Hence the restyle – and later I'm having a manicure.'

She giggles girlishly. A manicure.

I remember her calling my name. 'Stand up, Linda! Did I see you just then biting your nails? Come here.'

Out to the front of the class again.

'Disgusting!' she says. 'I say, everyone, Linda Denton eats fingernails for breakfast!'

Peals of nervous laughter. I pull myself back to the present. I towel dry her hair dry and select my scissors. I pick up sections of her hair as I'd been taught and snip away.

'Of course,' Miss Hartner says, 'they all begged me to stay, but I'd made my mind up. They struggled to find a replacement, I can tell you. When I announced my departure, the children were inconsolable. It's such a wrench for the poor loves. That's the hardest part about working with little ones. They grow attached to you.'

Really? I remember when I was in Year 6 and

some of the girls made friends with me, I discovered they were terrified of her too. Each had a tale to tell. Sonya told me how once when Miss Hartner shouted at her in class, she wet herself. So we made a little model of Miss Hartner and stuck pins into it. It didn't work, though.

I carried on snipping.

'I never married, you know. No time. I'm the sort of woman who dedicates herself to her career. But now I have time on my hands, who knows? The staff were suggesting I go on one of those single cruises.'

And drown yourself, I thought vindictively, feeling the scissors in my hand as weapon.

'I have to admit that I've been successful in my working life. It's no small achievement to be head of a prestigious school, especially for a single woman. I shall be telling the staff that in my speech tonight, so I can be an inspiration to them.'

One day she was patrolling our desks, watching us write a story. I could feel her homing in on me. I tried to make myself invisible but it didn't work.

'Linda Denton! You've been doodling on your story! I cannot believe it.'

In fact it wasn't a doodle – I'd been trying to draw a picture to go with the story. Some children got lost in a storm and ended up in another world where everything was upside-down and inside-out. And children were the bosses of adults and we all had to eat cat food. I remember that story. But I was too scared to explain any of that to Miss Hartner. She held my work up to show the others.

'This is Linda Denton's attempt at literature,' she said, icily. 'You can all be my witnesses that young Linda will amount to nothing. A girl who can't follow orders is set to fail, to be a nobody. Mark my words.'

She dropped my book on my desk. Tears sprung to my eyes.

'She's turned on her taps again,' Miss Hartner remarked.

When you're young, you think everything is your fault. I really believed that there was something wrong with me. I daydreamed about fame and money, but knew it would never happen. And here I am, junior stylist at the OK Coral.

'Not too short,' Miss Hartner comments.

'Oh no?' I think, and lift a section of her hair at the back. On a savage impulse, I lop the whole lot off. A rush of adrenaline hits me as I realise what I've done. How can I cover it up?

'Working with little ones keeps you youthful,'

Miss Hartner trills.

You self-deluding cow, I think, and chop off some more hair. Now there's a huge bald patch on the back of her head. I can't believe I'm doing this.

'In September I'm going to stay with my sister in Southport.'

Slowly and carefully, I remove section after section of hair from the back of her head. I wonder how much I can get away with before she notices what I'm doing. But she's oblivious, happily telling me how wonderful she is, thoroughly enjoying having an appreciative audience. Or so she thinks.

I remove all the hair from the back of her head, leaving only stubble. Then with wild abandon, I come round to the side and begin on the front.

'The asymmetric look is in right now,' I tell her, my heart thudding with icy fear and the deep satisfaction of the justice-giver. I snip off all the hair from the right side of her head.

' I don't think...' she says, starting to look alarmed. 'Do you know what you're doing?'

'Oh yes,' I say, filling with a mixture of sublime joy and numbing terror. 'Yes, I do.' I take a section from the very top of her head, and cut it off with a snap of my scissors.

She looks scared now, unsure. I stand back.

She lifts her hand and feels the back of her head. She lets out one enormous and ear-splitting scream.

Coral comes rushing over.

'What the -?!!!!!!'

Miss Hartner is up from the chair now, twisting round, seeing how she'd been scalped. No, not scalped but made a complete and utter fool of. Exposed. Named and shamed with my secret weapon. Coral is trying to pacify her. Then she turns to me.

'Linda Denton!' she screeches, and at the sound of my name, Miss Hartner stops and stares at me. I see recognition in her eyes. I smile triumphantly.

'Linda Denton. You're fired. You leave as of now.'

'With pleasure,' I say. 'You can keep your stinking job. I'm going somewhere better.'

I march into the back room and get my things. As I leave the salon I turn and smile at them all. Out in the High Road the sun is shining – it's warm, fragrant July. I think the library is the first place to go. They'll know where I can get on a course that starts this September. I'm going to take those A levels I thought I'd never have a chance of passing. I fancy English, and something a bit challenging – politics, maybe. Or even philosophy. Then I'll go to uni.. I'll work, and I'll succeed, because now I know I've got the courage to do anything – anything – I want.

Who says revenge isn't sweet?

131

Author profile
Rosie Rushton

Rosie Rushton has been writing for teenagers
for over ten years and still hasn't managed to
discipline any of her characters. She invents
them, then they take over – which is why every
book is a constant source of amazement to her.

When she isn't shouting at her computer
screen, she enjoys walking, travelling, visiting
schools and playing with her three grandchildren.
She is currently studying to be a reader in the
Church of England and has a few more books
up her sleeve yet!

Her latest book, 'What a Week to Take a
Chance', was published in September 2004.

The Kiss

by Rosie Rushton

I shouldn't have done it.

I wouldn't have done it if I'd known what would happen.

But at the time, saving my own skin was all I cared about. I thought they'd kill me if I didn't do it.

Now, with what's happened, I wish they had.

I wasn't going to tell anyone the whole story but I have to. If I don't, I'll go mad.

It happened yesterday, but it started weeks before. I've always been the odd one out at Mallen Park High and it's not just because of the scars. OK, so my face is lopsided, my skin's the colour of rusty drainpipes and my upper lip is almost invisible – that's because my big sister played with matches when she was three and my buggy caught fire with me strapped in it. To start with, I kind of compensated for that by larking around, learning to pull weird faces and act the fool in class and make guys laugh. It had worked at primary school and I guess I was dumb enough to think it would work forever.

It didn't. It wasn't that I expected anyone to be best mates with me at the new school – I don't play sport because the skin on my feet has gone all funny and even when I'm hooting with laughter, my face doesn't look happy. I can't do many expressions except frowns and my version of a contorted smile.

It doesn't mean I don't feel things though.

It was halfway through last term that they started laying into me. Spike and his gang, I mean. Not that you'd have noticed; they didn't clobber me one, or nick my stuff – well, not to start with anyway. They called me names – Ugly Face, Lipless, Freak Features – and they'd grab my books and fling them over the wall. That sort of stuff. Maybe it would have stayed that way. If only I'd been thick, or just off sick that day last term, maybe none of this would have happened.

It was Science and Mr. Conway had got us all doing experiments. What he does is, he grabs one of you and drags you to the front of class, and then uses you as a kind of assistant in the experiment. It was my turn that day: I'd been dumb enough to get an A* for my last assignment and this was supposed to be my reward. Duh. Anyway, he'd just got started, and he struck a match, the chemical in the test tube (can't even remember what it was now) crackled and flamed and I screamed. Well, actually I did more than that–I yelled and belted out of the room. God, I'm blushing just remembering – well, I know I'm blushing. You wouldn't be able to tell the difference. The thing is, I can't remember the fire in the baby buggy, but Dad reckons my body cells do. I see a flame and alarm bells ring all over my body. I won't even go near a barbecue and on Bonfire Night I just sit indoors with my headphones on real loud.

You have to give old Conners credit – he didn't make a scene. Just told me afterwards that he was sorry and he hadn't been thinking. Muttered a lot about the school counsellor and aversion therapy. Not that I haven't tried all that already. But from that minute on, Spike and his lot had me just where they wanted me. On the way home that afternoon, they cornered me by the allotments that run along the lane at the back of our estate and Karl, Spike's right hand thug, whipped out a box of matches. Luke and Adam pinned me up against the fence, and Spike snatched the matches from Karl, struck one and held it up to my face.

'See this?' he snarled, chewing on a piece of gum and waving the flame millimetres from my right eye. 'I'm gonna take out your eyelashes with this.'

I could feel the heat – you wouldn't think one little match could make you hot all over but it did. I felt my legs turn to water and I had a violent desire to do a pooh.

'Well?' Spike spat in my face. 'Yes or no?'

'Wh...wha...what d'ya mean?' I stammered, my heart pounding in my ears so loudly that I could hardly hear my own voice.

'Burning – or doing what we say?' Karl interjected.

I didn't reply. I thought if I opened my mouth, I'd spew my guts up all over his feet. I thought if I just hung on, someone would come down the path and stop them.

Spike twisted my left wrist behind my back.

'More!' he hissed at Karl.

I fought. I promise you I did. I turned my head, I kicked out with my feet, I even tried to wrench my elbow round and knock the matches from Karl's hand. But as the flame of the fourth match touched the eyelashes of my left eye, I screamed. Over and over.

'OK, OK, I'll do anything – OK, stop it – please, I'll do it, whatever it is.'

'I think,' Spike said, letting go of my wrists and spitting his gum onto the path, 'we've got a result.'

And that's how it started. At first it was nicking fags, then they wanted booze as well. Between you and me, the first few times I didn't steal from shops – I took cigarettes from Mum's handbag (I knew she wouldn't say a word, because Dad goes ballistic if he finds her smoking) and I nabbed a couple of bottles of Scotch from Dad's drinks cabinet. It's only there for when my grandparents come and I figured that was weeks away.

But in the end, I had to do shops because Spike wanted stuff we never had at home. I went to Mr Patel's down the corner of our street; he likes me and lets me amble around looking at the magazines and sussing the videos for rent, so I figured he wouldn't be watching me all the time, the way he eyes other kids up and down. And all the time I felt sick and the words 'Thief, thief,' kept rattling round in my head. Then last week, just as I was going out of the shop with a couple of packets of Marlborough Lights up my sleeve, Mr Patel shouted 'Hey you!' and I belted down the street, round the corner and then threw up and got regurgitated shepherds pie all down my trouser leg.

I didn't sleep that night and the next morning I was sick again and Mum kept me home. Then I started having nightmares and stomach cramps as well. At first, the doctor said it was a 'non-specific virus' which meant he hadn't got a clue what was wrong with me. Then he decided it was all in my mind, and I wasn't really ill at all, just unhappy. He asked all those usual dumb, doctor type questions – 'Anything bothering you?' (Like, you want a list?) and 'You can always talk about your problems, you know.' (Oh sure, and then get beaten up by Spike for dumping him in it. Get real.) Anyway, I was off school for three weeks and when I went back, there was this new girl in my class.

The moment I saw her, I knew what all those love songs were about. You can laugh – I don't care. Better you laugh about me falling in love than about my ugly face. Shelby, her name was. Is. She'd come to our town from Great Falls – that's in Montana which is in America – because her father was working on some project at the Open University.

'Hi,' she said to me that first morning at break. Just like that. 'Hi.' It may be no big deal to you, but then you probably look normal. Most people either look away when they first meet me, or else go to the other extreme and start dashing about offering me seats and smiling sickly sweet smiles to prove just how good they are with disabled people. Shelby didn't do anything like that. She just spoke to me like I was ordinary.

'Hi,' I replied.

'Are you better?' she asked.

'Better than what, exactly?' I grinned.

And she laughed. Not the horrid, embarrassed laugh at my lopsided lips but a real, throw back your head kind of laugh.

'That's cool,' she chuckled. 'Want a chocolate brownie?'

And that's how we started. Sounds good, doesn't it – 'we'. I'd never been part of a 'we' before. It was just mates, of course; nothing hands on or slushy, but it was nice. She wasn't in my sets what with having come from America and not knowing any European history or French or stuff. But at lunch times and in free periods, we hung out and talked and it was cool.

Till Spike and his lot noticed us.

'We've got a job for you, Freak Features,' Spike said, swaggering up to us at lunch time last Wednesday. 'Adam here is having a party and we need booze, right, Ads?'

'Yeah,' nodded Adam, whose vocabulary is limited at the best of times.

'So get it,' Spike said, looking not at me but at Shelby whose eyes were widening by the minute. 'Or else.'

'Chris,' Shelby demanded after the gang had moved off, 'what was that guy on about?'

'Him?' I shrugged. 'Oh, my Dad runs an off licence and he lets my mates have a discount on...'

My lies didn't cut ice with her.

'They're thirteen,' she stressed. 'You don't drink when you're thirteen.'

'Not in America, maybe,' I floundered. 'But here, in your own homes...'

'Chris Matthews, I'm not a fool,' she drawled. 'They want you to steal it, right?'

'Get real,' I replied. 'What do you take me for? A thief? Well, thanks very much!'

And with that, I stomped off across the school yard.

She didn't look at me for the rest of the day. Or the next day.

'Got the booze?' Spike said to me at lunch break.

'No,' I said flatly. 'I'm not getting any more.'

I clenched my teeth together to stop them chattering and tried to imagine I was some kind of cross between James Bond and Superman.

They couldn't do much about it right then because Mr Connors was on playground duty and he's got eyes in the back of his head, but they made up for it after school. They pinned me on the ground and they kicked me and gave me Chinese burns and then lit a match and singed the ends of my hair.

That's when I flipped. I screamed and shouted and yelled 'Help' over and over until Adam clamped his sweaty palm over my mouth.

'Wait!' Spike's tone was assertive enough to make the other two stop their battering. 'Got an idea.'

Had I been capable of any sort of witty remark, I'd have said there was a first time for everything, but I was fighting for breath and I'd just wet myself and was desperate not to let it show.

'You like Shelby, right?' Spike said, casting a wary eye down the path towards a couple of women walking their dogs.

'She's OK,' I mumbled, licking the blood on my lip and wincing at the pain.

'This is what you're going to do,' Spike said. 'Kiss her.'

'What?' The thought of kissing Shelby had been racing through my mind for days but the reality was a non-starter. I can't even do the kiss shape in the mirror, never mind for real.

'And we'll time you, Lipless' Spike said. 'One minute, you get one day's respite from working for us, two minutes equals two days...'

By then they were all choking with laughter, punching one another on the shoulder as if they'd just come up with the answer to world peace.

'Tomorrow. After school, behind the sports pavilion.' Spike ordered. 'Be there or die.'

I didn't believe him. Even bullies like him don't go around killing people. I knew that. But I wasn't quite ready to put it to the test.

'Shelby,' I said first thing the following morning, 'I need to talk to you.'

'To say what?' she asked abruptly. 'How good you are at nicking stuff?'

'No,' I answered quickly. 'I'll never do that again as long as I live, honest.'

She eyed me closely.

'You mean it?'

'Sure,' I said, stepping closer. 'It was dumb. It's just that when you look a freak like me...'

'You don't look a freak and if you wallow in self pity, I'm not hanging around,' she declared. 'Now what did you want to talk about?'

So I told her.

'And you, Chris Matthews, want me to kiss you just because those arseholes told you to? Well, thank you for nothing!'

She turned and flounced off. I ran after her.

'It's not that – well, I mean it is that, but it's not like I don't want to. I do want to but ..'

'You do?'

I nodded miserably.

'There's no point anyway. I can't do it. I don't know how.'

'Right,' she said firmly. 'Where is this charade supposed to take place?'

I told her.

'Be there,' she said.

If only I hadn't been so relieved, if only I hadn't been such a coward, if only I'd told someone....all

142

the 'if onlys' in the world won't change a thing.

At four o'clock, we got to the Sports Pavilion. Spike and the gang were there – and so were about fifty other kids.

'So what are you all staring at?' Shelby demanded at the top of her voice. 'We're not going to do anything so you might as well push off.'

My heart missed a beat, whether from relief at not having to make a fool of myself or fear of reprisals, I'm not too sure.

Spike, Adam and Karl took a couple of steps closer.

'Do it or die' Spike hissed.

'By fire,' added Adam.

'Slowly,' sniggered Karl.

That's when I saw the fireworks. They were sticking out of Spike's pocket – the ones called Flame Thrower that get lit and explode and shoot blue and yellow flames out at all angles.

'I'll do it,' I said hastily.

'No,' gasped Shelby. 'Don't give in to them. Stand up for yourself. What are you? A wimp?'

I hesitated. I mean, I knew I was a wimp, but I knew I loved Shelby and suddenly I wanted her to admire me.

But by then, Karl had handed Spike the matches. Spike stuck a firework in the ground a couple of centimetres from my foot. Karl lit a match.

'Kiss!' shouted Spike 'or we light it.'

'Kiss, kiss, kiss,' the crowd of kids took up the chant.

My heart racing, I leaned towards Shelby and tried desperately to pucker my lips. I knew by the roar of laughter that puckering was not my strong point.

I've relived the next bit over and over in my mind. I saw Shelby's eyes widen in horror, and I guessed that it was having my hideous face so close to hers that did it. But then, out of the corner of my half open eye I saw the sparks, saw that Karl had lit the firework.

'Move!' Shelby shouted, pushing me out of the way.

She shoved me to one side and I stumbled against the wall of the Sports Pavilion. She darted towards the firework, stretched out a hand.

'Noooo!' I yelled.

But it was too late.

I threw myself on top of her, rolled her over and over on the grass, ripped off my shirt and beat out the flames.

'That was so brave,' the paramedic said when the ambulance finally arrived.

But it wasn't.

144

I was scared stiff. But I thought that if she died, I wanted to as well. And if she was going to have a scarred face, or burned hands, then I wanted to have something worse. As a punishment.

They've said I can see her in a bit. They brought me into the hospital as well to check me over and when they saw the bruises on my ribs they called Mum and Dad and they cried and I had to tell them about Spike because the nurse was looking at them all funny and I knew what they were thinking. Of course, I didn't mention Spike by name. Wimp I may be: dumb I'm not.

Mum and Dad have gone to the café to get me a sandwich. Not that I can eat it, but it gets them out of the way for a bit.

'Hi!'

It's her. I can't look. I can't turn round. I've ruined her face. It's all my fault. If I had stood up to Spike....

'Thanks, Chris.'

'For what?' I spit the words out, still not daring to look at her.

'Saving me,' she says and her hand brushes mine. No bandages on her hand at least, which is one good thing I guess.

'Hey, you,' she says. 'How long are you going to keep me waiting?'

'For what?' I mumble, furious at the tears

which are filling my eyes and threatening to spill over.

'My kiss,' she says softly.

Slowly, holding my breath, I turn. Her face is as lovely as ever, even though there is a big bruise on her left cheek and a large bandage on her neck. Her right hand is bandaged as well. My fault.

She is smiling.

'It's OK,' she says. 'I've got a couple of burns on my legs and a small one on my right arm but nothing much. The hand's the worst and even that'll be fine in a few months they say. Thanks to you - you put the fire out so fast.'

'I did?' She looks all wobbly but I think that's because my eyes are wet.

She nods. She is holding my hand. She is pulling me towards her.

Closer.

And closer.

You know something? This kissing business isn't half as hard as people make out.

Author profile
Grace Dent

Grace Dent started to write 'lots of depressing poetry and short stories' when she was in the sixth form but began to write properly when she was studying English Literature at Stirling University.

Since then she has written for the Guardian, the Mirror and Sunday Mirror as well as Cosmo Girl, Shape and More!

Her latest book 'LBD: The Great Escape' was published in July 2004.

Saved by a Whisper
by Grace Dent

'I just sort of, need some, er, y'know, space,' he mutters, rather sheepishly.

'You what?' I squeak, two octaves above calm. Maybe I've misheard him? Sometimes he speaks too softly to understand. My right hand grips my mobile phone clammily.

'What d'you mean space?!' I say, 'I don't underst...'

'Look, Kari, I don't think we should be together any more!' he blurts out.

He sounds almost vexed. He sounds like he's the one being dumped!

'Oh...' I grunt. Then I don't say anything. Neither does he.

The silence is gruesome.

Outside, Mum mows the lawn into neatly-coiffeured stripes. Across the landing, my big sister Jess titivates her hair for a night out at Legends Nightclub. Inside this bedroom, my life has dissolved into a large pile of poo. I don't think I've felt so distraught since Dad picked me up from the Year 10 Summer disco wearing tight acrylic shorts and a fisherman's hat. That almost induced suicide.

'Look, I've gotta, y'know go,' he mutters. 'Got, y'know, plans. I'm doing something with the lads. I'll see you round sometime, eh?'

'Plans!' I explode, 'We had plans! Tonight! You horrible pig! You were taking me to see Zombie Explosion III! I've been pruning my eyebrows and pushing back my cuticles since five o' clock!' My kohl eye-makeup has formed rivulets down my face, I look like an evil presence that has crawled from a crypt.

'Mmmm...soz about that...' he says, 'Gotta go...'

'Josh!' I plead, 'Don't just put the phone down on me! What have I done wr...Hey are you there? Josh!'

He's gone.

I sit on my bed, shaking with tears, totally bamboozled.

Ditched! Ditched by the gorgeous Josh Merton?! The four most blissful weeks of my life with Britain's most perfect boy ever, over in one abrupt call. I feel like lying behind the shed and asking Mum to trim my fringe with the Hover Mower. Ok, yes I know I should toughen up and take a more 'girl power' approach to rejection like Britney Spears or Christina Aguilera would.

(Perhaps I should change into leather hotpants and a silk bra and pirouette down Harold Street singing empowering songs about the stupidity of lads in general! That would show him!) Sadly it's taking all my strength to stop running over to Firtree Avenue, shinning the drainpipe before wrestling Josh to the floor, begging him for one last tongue-tackle.

Something tells me this wouldn't be very cool.

Tears are splish-sploshing down my cheeks, gurgling in the back of my throat. I'm a sniffling, snottery wretch of a chick. My saddest Avril Lavigne CD is blaring out, as I lie back and think about better times, such as watching Josh play five-a-side footie with the other Year 11 boys last week. Or snogging the most perfect snog just outside my front gate last Wednesday. Or even ten minutes ago, when I thought we were going to watch Zombies exploding.

That just makes me sob even more.

'What on earth's the matter?!' cries Mum, grabbing my hands, squatting in front of me. My primal moaning and snot flinging was evidently audible from even downstairs.

'Nothing. Go away!' I say.

No-one can make me feel better, there's no point in talking about it.

'Tell me,' instructs Mum, biting her lip, clearly

worried. 'There's been bad news?' she asks, lifting the soggy phone from my hands, 'Has there been an accident?'

'Joshghhhghgghh!' I snort, blowing my brains into a paper hankie.

'Shloosh?!' she repeats.

'He finishedpgghh with me!' I say.

Mum peers at me, before pulling an expression usually reserved for when she finds my brother's crusty bogeys stuck to the sofa.

'What? That Josh boy finished with you!?' she gasps, 'Flipping cheek!'

Mum gathers me up in a clumsy hug. She smells of compost and Estee Lauder body-moisturer. It feels lovely, although I'd never admit that. I'm almost 15 now, not a baby!

'Flipping cheek!' she says again, 'Ooh, he's got some nerve! He's having a laugh, he is!'

'Why?' I sniff.

'The mumbler! That's what we call him! Couldn't make out a word he ever said. It was like listening to the Shipping Forecast on a badly tuned radio.'

'Eh?' I say, dumbfounded. I thought that made him mysterious!

'You never said you didn't like him!' I say.

'Oh I didn't dare, that would have just made you more determined to date him,' says Mum, craftily. 'But now, the gloves are off!'

'He's quite shy,' I say, defending him.

'Shy?! Hah!?' she huffs, 'There's a very thin line between shy and rude, Kari. He pole-vaulted that right into arrogant.'

'But...he,' I stutter.

I should never have told Mum that last week he said I had 'quite chunky thighs'.

'And he had a shifty look about him,' Mum adds triumphantly, passing me more tissues, 'One eye was looking at you, one was looking at the door! He looked like a Crimewatch photofit!'

Mum's laughing now, her green eyes twinkle infectiously, tempting me to join her.

'He did not!' I protest, trying to forget the many times over the last months when he's behaved rather oddly. Disappeared for days on end, phone switched off, no explanations. Suzy and Tanya, my two bestest friends, have hinted they think that he's shady, but would I listen to them? Oh dear, I wish I'd phoned them a bit more over the last month whilst I've been lost in the magic of love. I bet they're not speaking to me now. I could really do with them here too.

'Ok, he could be a bit odd sometimes,' I admit, beginning to cry again, 'But he was totally and utterly gorgeous, wasn't he, Mum? He was like a male model!'

As Mum ruffles my hair and mops my tears, the bedroom door swings open. Nobody knocks in

153

this house ever. It drives me mad.

'Who's like a male model!?' announces Dad, smiling 'Come on now ladies, you know I don't like being talked about.'

'Leave it, Frank, we're having a crisis!' says Mum, holding one hand up.

'Ooh what's happened?' he asks nosily.

My dad loves gossip. Despite his hairy nose and love of Grand Prix, he'd make an excellent woman.

'It's 'The Mumbler',' frowns Mum. 'He's dumped her.'

'Who?!' says Dad,

'The lad who mumbles! Shifty eyes!' says Mum, cupping her hand around her mouth as if that'll stop me hearing.

'What! Rodent boy!' tuts Dad, 'He dumped my beautiful little princess! Pah! You're well rid there Kari, petal. Hey, did you ever notice how small and pink his hands and head were as compared to his body?'

'I thought that too!' nods Mum, merrily.

'Will you two please leave my bedroom now,' I request, pointlessly.

'No, hang on, don't get cross,' chuckles Dad,

'I'm just saying he had extraordinarily small pink hands. He reminded me of a weird mutant human/hamster cross-species! I found him quite...eerie!'

'I thought he was really handsome!' I sulk, realising that this now sounds a little ridiculous.

'Like a younger Orlando Bloom!'

'Oh sure!' scoffs Dad, 'He was a right looker! Scurrying around with that twitchy nose. He looked like he should be running on one of those big wheels. And those baggy trousers hanging off his bum all the time. Could he not afford a belt?' Mum's really laughing now.

I give my father a stern look. He has no room to speak about anyone's fashion sense, being the only man in Britain who'd wear a lime-coloured quilted anorak.

'You're far too good for him!' says Dad.

'Too good for who?' says Jess, striding into my room, stealing my hair lacquer and scooshing her hair before staring at me oddly, 'Jeez Kari, what happened to your face? You going Trick or Treating?'

'I split up with Josh,' I sigh.

'Who?' she says.

'Y'know Josh?' says Dad, 'The one we were talking about!' Dad mimes something rodenty with long whiskers eating a piece of cheese.

'Never met him,' says Jess, stealing my pink lipgloss.

Jess might as well use it. I won't be going anywhere for a long, long time.

'You know? The mumbler!' mimics Mum, crossing her eyes, 'Y'know mpghhhgg mpghghghg?'

'Oh him?! The lad with the big voluminous spot on his neck!' smiles Jess.

I cringe. Josh did have a pluke the size of Denmark for a fortnight of our torrid love tryst. I didn't mind at the time, even though I had to kiss around the yellow part. Yeuch! That's disgusting! I can't believe I did that.

'Right everyone out! And I mean it!' I say, leaping up and shooing my family out of my room. I need some me-time to wallow in this misery. I want to torture myself thinking about the wonderful boyfriend I've let slip through my fingers. Life will never be the same, after that phone-call.

However annoyingly, every time I think about Josh now, I visualise an enormous fieldmouse, with wonky eyes wearing massive trousers, mumbling all of his words from behind a radioactive zit on his neck!

So I've had my long bubble bath (prepared by Mum using all her most expensive bath oils) and Jess has kindly lent me her DVD player plus a stack of funny DVDs. I'm feeling much brighter. Especially as Tanya and Suzy are perched on beanbags on my bedroom floor, munching

Maltesers, listening to the whole unfolding saga.

'Chunky thighs!' scoffs Tanya. ' Pah! Nonsense! Good riddance to him! Never liked him anyway.'

'I never had a clue what he was saying either,' says Suzy, 'He was always mumbling! Was he speaking Urdu or something?'

'Gnnngnnn.' I groan.

I take out my only photo of my ex-boyfriend, an old passport booth snap that he graciously said I could have.

'Tell me something girls,' I say, passing them the photo, 'Do you think there's something a bit, well, rodenty, about Josh?'

Tanya stares at the picture before bursting into fits of giggles. I can't help joining in.

'Oh yeah!' Suzy squeals, 'It's those small pink hands and pointy nose! He could be the starring role in Honey I Blew Up the Gerbil!'

Suzy laughs so hard she falls headfirst off her beanbag, sitting up with a chocolate stuck to her forehead. This makes us all howl even more. I'd not realised how much I missed them. I never laughed like this with Josh.

As Suzy loads American Pie into the DVD player then raids my dressing table for nail-varnish, Tanya is jabbering on about a dress she spotted today in Miss Selfridge she reckons would suit me.

'It's a bias cut, with pink flowers down the

front,' says Tanya, 'It's got dainty little spaghetti straps. It's so totally you, Kari! You could wear it for Tina Jessop's 15th birthday party next week.'

'Which you must come to, Kari,' stresses Liza, 'Cos there's going to be loads of lush boys there!' I look at them both a bit apprehensively.

I'm not ready for partying just yet.

Then suddenly my mobile phone begins to vibrate. Josh Calling...flashes upon the screen, accompanied by a rather flattering J-Peg of the boy himself. Josh's eyes do look exceedingly blue on that picture. He's smiling at me. My stomach lurches. Tanya and Suzy look at each other apprehensively. I take a deep breath, then press 'Answer'.

'Hello?' I say

'Alright?' says Josh.

There's an awkward silence.

'What can I do for you?' I say.

'Well, mmm... y'know,' mutters Josh, 'I've been..mmm...thinking. Maybe I shouldn't have dumped you before? Cos, like, I was just in a bad mood, y'see? I started thinking that I couldn't be bothered having a girlfriend.'

'Sorry, beg your pardon, Josh?' I say 'Could you say that again? You're mumbling.'

It takes me all my nerve to do this, but it feels brilliant. Tanya and Suzy gasp.

'So I thought,' Josh says, speaking more

audibly, 'That..mmm... I'd give you another chance. Cos, y'know, you're not that bad.'

'What's he saying!' Tanya's mouthing.

I put my hand over the phone.

'He says I'm not that bad. He'll give me another chance.'

Suzy's eyes glint furiously. I take another deep breath.

'I don't think so, Josh.' I tell him firmly. 'In fact, don't call ever call me again.'

Down the line, I hear a sharp intake of breath.

'You what!?' snaps Josh. 'You ungrateful cow! I'm giving you another chance here. Don't you understand me?'

'Sorry? Pardon,' I say, 'You're mumbling again.' The girls are both laughing really hard now.

'Now listen here, Josh, there's no need to get ratty about this,' I say, innocently.

Lisa has to bite one of my pillows to stop herself squealing.

'I know you think you're the big cheese around school,' I continue, 'But you'll just have to scurry off now. It's over.'

'But!' he says, 'But!'

I hang up on him. Then switch the phone off entirely. I'm shaking, but I feel good.

'Now then Tanya,' I say, feeling much more like my old self, 'That party dress. What colour was it exactly.'

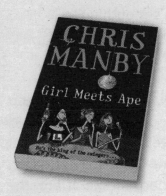

Author profile
Chris Manby

Chris Manby grew up in Gloucester and published her first short story in J17 while she was still at school. Fifteen years later, she is the author of eight best-selling romantic comedy novels and editor of two chart-topping short story collections for War Child, 'Girls' Night In and 'Boys' Night In / Girls' Night Out'.

   She lives between London and Los Angeles. Her latest novel, 'Girl Meets Ape', was published in August 2004.

The Journey
by Chris Manby

No-one could have been happier than I was when Mum got herself a new boyfriend. But after a couple of months with Olivier, she was starting to develop some pretty embarrassing verbal tics. For example, she never said 'OK' anymore. Instead she said, 'Hip-cool, oui.' Coming from Olivier with his great French accent, it was hip-cool indeed. Coming from Mum, it was just a bit sad.

Anyway, it was getting close to the summer holidays. Normally, I would have gone and stayed with Dad but that year he had been promoted at work and had to spend two months digging in the dust in Saudi Arabia. Mum didn't want me to go there. I definitely didn't want to go there. So I had to go on holiday with her and Olly instead.

'You are so lucky,' said my best friend Emma. 'Two weeks in the South of France. Two weeks with a French boy!'

Oh yeah. Olly's godson from Paris was coming too. Axel was his name. He was going to catch the train across country and meet us in the seaside town near St. Tropez where Olly had

grown up. Axel was sixteen. I was fourteen.
Emma predicted the perfect opportunity to
improve international relations.

'Axel!' Olly shouted down the platform.

I scanned the passengers getting off the train
for my future French husband, making sure I
looked as good as possible for the moment when
we first locked eyes. You have no idea how long it
took me to get ready that morning. I wore an
outfit I bought with the money Dad sent to make
up for the fact I wouldn't be holidaying with him.
Great jeans, a cute top. A pair of shoes that were
killing my feet...

'Axel!'

Eventually, there was no-one left on the
platform but me, Mum, Olly and one super-
gorgeous French boy. His clothes were great. His
hair was great. His face was great. And, be still
my beating heart, he was a nice guy with it. He
was actually helping some poor guy in a
wheelchair with his bags.

'Hey, Olly!'

A poor guy in a wheelchair who was addressing
my future step-father by name...

The gorgeous boy walked straight past us and
into the arms of his waiting girlfriend.

'Axel, this is Seema.' Olly introduced me to the
cripple.

'Nice shoes,' said Axel.

I glanced down at his feet, dressed in what appeared to be a cross between 1970's platforms and medieval torture instruments, and felt more than a little bit weird.

So much for my fantasy that I'd spend the next two weeks floating along the beach in the company of a dashing French god, listening to compliments drop from his lips in that fabulous accent until I couldn't stop myself from hurling him onto the sand and covering him with kisses.

There was to be no floating along the beach with Axel. Olly had to carry him down the steps and across the sand to the island of beach blankets Mum set up every morning. He stayed there all day, in the shade of an umbrella, reading piles of books or talking to the grown-ups. He didn't even have to get up to go to the bathroom because he had some kind of bag attached to his kidneys, I think.

The holiday was turning out to be a disaster. Mum wasn't happy for me to go very far on my own and Axel couldn't come anywhere with me. I read all the books I'd brought with me in the first three days. Axel offered to read me some of his poetry.

'I think he was trying to flirt with me,' I told Emma when I called her that night.

'Oh, yuck,' said Emma. 'That really is gross.'

I began to think I might have been better

off in Saudi.

On the fourth day, I rebelled. I told Mum that I wasn't going to the beach that day. I was going to stay in the villa. On my own.

'You can't stay on your own all day,' she replied.

'I'm fourteen', I reminded her.

'I still think of you as thirteen and four quarters. I can't leave you here by yourself.'

'I'll stay with her,' said Axel.

'An excellent idea,' said Olly. He whispered something in my mother's ear that made her giggle and agree.

So now I was stuck in the villa with the crip.

'You don't like me, do you?' said Axel when Mum and Olly had gone.

'Of course I like you,' I snorted back.

'Then why won't you look at me?' he asked. 'Perhaps it's because you fancy me. That's usually why a girl won't look at a guy.'

'Oh, dream on,' I said. 'You're a cripple.' I regretted that immediately.

'You know, it's just my legs that don't work,' said Axel. 'Everything in here is perfectly functional.' He tapped his head. 'And here,' he tapped his heart. 'I was looking forward to spending a couple of weeks with an English girl. I thought we might have something to learn from each other. But these last few days, I've begun to wonder whether there's anything I want to know about you at all. You read crappy magazines. You listen to terrible music. You talk to your mother like she's your servant. You haven't made the effort to say a single word of French...'

'Encollez-vous,' I spat at him.

'What? You want me to go paste myself?' Axel sneered at me. 'You don't even know enough French to swear.'

We spent the rest of the morning at opposite ends of the house. Me, scribbling furiously in my diary. Axel...A familiar fragrance reached my nose. I leaned out of the window of my bedroom to see Axel on the patio. He was smoking.

'That's a disgusting habit,' I shouted to him.

'Goes with the rest of me,' Axel shouted back

He didn't look at me but the tone of his voice let me know exactly how he felt. I was feeling pretty rubbish myself. After all, he'd just told me I was stupid, uncultured and ignorant. I didn't want to be that girl. And I certainly didn't want Mum to come back and find out we had been arguing.

I walked out of the villa and sat on the back step beside Axel in his wheelchair.

'We need to make up,' I said. 'Mum gets really upset if people row.'

'Olly doesn't like it either.'

165

'It wasn't your wheelchair that made me weird with you,' I said. 'You just seem like such a genius with all those books.'

Axel offered me a drag on his cigarette.

'But not such a genius that you're clever enough not to smoke.'

I smiled and pushed the fag away.

The holiday got much better after that. Axel convinced Olly and Mum that we could look after ourselves. Each morning, Olly drove us to a part of town where Axel could use his chair then disappeared with Mum to get romantic. Axel and I spent long afternoons hanging together outside a cafe on the town square. He told me about the birth defect that had twisted his legs. I told him about Mum and Dad's divorce. He told me about the kids who picked on him because he wasn't able-bodied. I told him about the kids who picked on me because my grandparents came from Mumbai. I taught him the proper lyrics to a Blink 182 song he had been singing wrong for a year. He taught me how to order a glass of wine in perfect French. Not that we did, of course.

And pretty soon, I didn't see the chair when I looked at my friend. I saw his brown eyes, his passably trendy hair cut. I saw the way his mouth curled up in a smile when I got my French pronunciation wrong.

On our last night in the villa, Mum and Olly

went out, leaving me and Axel to eat French bread and cheese beneath an olive tree. It was a perfectly clear night. I don't think I'd ever seen so many stars before, having grown up beneath the artificial orange glow of London. Axel pointed out some constellations to me. I crouched on the ground next to his wheelchair to better see where he was pointing. He patted the arm of the chair, inviting me to perch there. When he finished describing the stars, he tipped his head back and looked up at the sky. He sighed.

'I've had such a good holiday,' he said.

'And me,' I said honestly. 'With you.'

For the first time since we made friends, Axel and I found ourselves in another uncomfortable silence. But this time, I knew what I wanted to do to fill it.

'Can I kiss you?' I asked him then.

'No,' he said.

'It's not because I feel sorry for you,' I assured him. 'It's not because I want to tell my friends I kissed a guy in a wheelchair or anything. I just... I just want to kiss you, Axel.'

'No,' said Axel. 'I don't want you to.'

I stared at him. 'Why not?'

'Perhaps I just don't fancy you,' he said.

When he finished laughing, Axel pulled me from the arm of the wheelchair and onto his lap. He wrapped his arms around me and rested his cool

cheek against mine. He did kiss me then. But
only like you would have kissed a baby.

'Friends forever', he told me.

'Bien sur', I said. 'Amis toujours'.

Author profile
Karen McCombie

Before writing full-time, Karen worked for several teen magazines such as J17 and Sugar in a variety roles - everything from fashion to features!

There are now fourteen titles in her highly successful 'Ally's World' series. An 'Ally's World' Journal will be available for Christmas 2004.

'Marshmallow Magic and the Wild Rose Rouge', her latest novel, was published in hardback in August 2004.

When not writing Karen spends her time belly-dancing!

The Sweetest White Lie
by Karen McCombie

My dad got me the job. Mum didn't speak to him
for a week after.

'But Pete, will it be safe! She'll be miles away!'
she demanded of Dad (er, before she stopped
talking to him).

'Sarah, it's just for one day,' my dad replied
wearily. 'Mike is going to take Evie there, and
take her back. He'll be with her the whole time.
And she'll be working with other girls her age.
She'll be fine.'

Speaking about my age, I'm fifteen, though
you'd be forgiven for thinking I'm five, the way
my mum goes on.

She can't help it; she's not just over-protective,
she's hyper-protective. Thank God for mobile
phones; if I didn't have one to call my mum on,
she'd have a fit every time I mooched around
and chatted to my friends for ten minutes after
school or whatever.

'Your mother's got such a wild imagination, she
should have been a writer instead of an optician,'
Dad said with a wicked grin, after this one time

171

my calling credit ran out and Mum flipped 'cause I was quarter of an hour late back from Katie's house. In that quarter of an hour, she'd managed to convince herself that I'd probably eloped with a sixty-year-old bearded bricklayer called Eddie who I'd met in a chatroom masquerading as a fourteen-year-old Phixx fan...

Because my mum is on the nice side of normal in every other way, I decided long ago not to get too wound up about her bad habit of assuming the world is populated almost entirely by weirdos lurking in bushes outside my school, or gangs of teenage thugs who want to get me hooked on drugs, or run me over in the cars they're joy-riding around in when they're not selling drugs.

And irritating as it is to have to check in with her all the time, at least it's kind of nice (in an annoying way) to know she cares. Ever since Katie's mum got all loved up with her new boyfriend a few weeks ago, she's been acting like the worst delinquent you've ever met, regularly reeling in at two in the morning, reeking of pub. Katie says that at the moment she could hold an all-night illegal rave in the living room, paint pentagrams on the kitchen units and get a spiderweb tattoo on her face and her mother wouldn't notice; she's too busy teetering into the house in her sexiest heels, in a waft of cigarette smoke and gin fumes, humming Dido songs and whispering giggled night-nights to someone called Georgiou on her mobile.

'At least your mum notices you're there,' Katie grumbled to me the other day. 'I get about as much attention as the cheeseplant at the moment...'

Yep. My mum notices alright, to the point where I feel like I'm under a microscope half the time. Actually, I'd been quite looking forward to today – not just 'cause Dad's mate Mike said he was going to pay me £40 for my efforts (those new jeans from Gap, coming right up!), but because for eight hours solid, I'd be working, and Mum couldn't expect me to check in with her, could she?

Could she?

'Hi Evie... everything alright?'

'Mum, it's fine!' I hiss, tucking the phone between my shoulder and my chin, as I try to serve the customer in front of me, and not panic at the size of the never-ending queue behind him. 'I told you it was fine last time you called!'

'Oh, yes, sorry. You know me; I just thought I'd say hi and see how you were doing.'

Honestly, I don't know what's going through Mum's head, but I can kind of guess: she'll be having visions of me being pestered by hardened crack dealers, or strange middle-aged men offering to show me pictures of puppies if I just step into their cars. Mum doesn't seem to get it, those sort of people don't really hang around at Steam Engine & Tractor Rallies in country parks. And even if by some strange coincidence they did, they wouldn't necessarily be queuing up for a slab of Rum'n'Raisin at Ye Olde Fudge Kitchen stall, where I happen to be working.

In fact, my only customers are endless little kids, bored with gawping at steam engines and desperate for a sugar hit, or elderly tractor fanatics who don't seem to mind the idea of welding their dentures together with a hefty hunk of Hazelnut 'n' Vanilla.

But just you try getting my certifiably paranoid mother to believe that.

'Mum, I'm supposed to be working! Listen, I've got to go – I'm getting a dirty look from Mike...'

That isn't quite true. There are a lot of people idly staring at me right now, but Mike isn't one of them. Still, I need to lean on a little white lie to get rid of Mum.

'Sorry, Evie, I didn't mean to get you into troub–'

I press the off button on her – my normally endless patience running out – and find myself handing the old bloke in front of me my phone, while I slip his change in my pocket. (Duh...)

Y'know, I'm seriously frazzled. Apart from Mum phoning me four times today already (on the way to the country park, once I'd arrived at the country park, half-way through the morning and just now), I've got a few problems...

First, out of the three girls that were supposed to be manning the fudge stall, there's now only me; one girl rang Dad's friend Mike this morning to say she couldn't make it. And then Zoe – who'd looked green since the moment we picked her up in the van – spent so long locked in the portable ladies' loos with a dodgy stomach that Mike had had to run her home before Ye Olde Fudge Kitchen customers complained of getting a free dose of salmonella with every purchase.

Second, Mike rang five minutes ago to say he'd run out of petrol on the way back to the Rally, and was stuck on a lay-by waiting for the AA, and could I manage alright for a while?

And thirdly, I need a wee really, really badly and have no idea how you can close a stall up when it doesn't exactly have a door, never mind a lock...

'Next, please!' I mutter, as I frantically swap my phone and the old bloke's change around.

God, I wish I'd spent the afternoon with Katie, window-shopping for things I can't afford, instead of slaving over some melting fudge, trying to do four people's jobs at once, dressed in a naff white overall two sizes too big and a lace-edged white bonnet that looks like a strange mating between

175

a shower cap and an antique tablecloth.

Could this day get any worse?

'Hey, Evie! What are you doing here?'

Yes, it could.

'Er... hi!' I stumble out a reply, finding myself talking to Danny Chopra.

You know how there are lads you can be quite friendly with, and have a laugh with in a crowd? But outside of that crowd, you realise you don't really know them that well, and end up with your mouth drier than sawdust and elephants trampling around in your stomach when you meet them?

Well, imagine that, then imagine you're wearing what I'm wearing. Now you know what hell is...

'Kind of a coincidence, huh?' Danny grins at me.

Out of school uniform, he looks pretty cute, or pretty cool, or pretty much both; I can't really tell 'cause I'm a bit flustered, knowing that I must look like I got dressed for a bet today.

'Wha– what are you doing here?' I manage to babble.

Like I say, I only sort of know Danny. He's in the year above me at school, but me and Katie often hang out with his sister Anita and her friends, and sometimes he'll come and chat with us all at breaktime. But even though I don't know him too well, I guess I had him down as more of a hip-hop and garage kind of guy, rather than a Steam Engine & Tractor Rally freak…

'I– I came with my cousin. He's kind of into all this… stuff,' says Danny, with a shrug.

Out of school uniform, he looks taller, leaner. I don't recognise the name of the band on the front of his T-shirt, but I know that that shade of grey-blue looks great against his light brown skin.

A cough from the woman standing behind Danny reminds us both that I don't have all day to stand around staring at Danny's general cuteness. I've got customers desperate to buy soggy fudge.

'So… can I get you something?' I ask Danny, trying to sound efficient.

'Um, yeah; some of that Choc-Chip fudge?' he says, pointing to a mound by my right elbow. The mound that I now knock flying with my elbow, and end up scrabbling about on the grass for, to the sound of giggles, sighs and tutting from the queue behind Danny.

Now that I'm down here, I don't think I want to straighten up. Maybe I'll just crawl on my hands and knees through the plastic checkered sheeting at the back of the stall, and try and hitch-hike my way back to town. (Mmm! Mum would love that!)

Only there're two legs in jeans suddenly blocking my escape route.

'Looks like the Choc-Chip's off the menu, then!'

grins Danny, bending down beside me and scooping up handfuls of grass-flecked fudge to toss in the bin. 'Listen, you serve – I'll help.'

And for the next hour and a half, Danny does nothing but help. He goes and gets me a sandwich, and serves while I gulp it down. He lets me nip (make that run) to the portable loos, and manages to charm a bunch of old ladies into buying all the fancy gift boxes of fudge by the time I come back. He carries on serving while I take a call from Mike, who's finally on the way back with the van, and who tells me I've done really well and will get a big, fat bonus (not a gift box of fudge, I hope).

'That was a laugh!' says Danny, as I turn around after serving the last customer, now that the crowds are dwindling and the rally's winding up.

'A laugh? It was a nightmare!' I grin at him, reaching up to straighten his fluffy, puffy, white hat.

It's official – I don't have elephants thundering around in my belly anymore when I look at Danny Chopra. You can't exactly stay shy with someone who you've been sharing a confined space with, giggling as you crash into each other, hands bashing together as you both reach for the same piece of Very Berry fudge. And you can't be shy of someone who's stuck on a hat that's as silly as yours, just to make the customers (and you) smile.

'Hey, I wouldn't exactly say it's been a nightmare...' says Danny softly.

My fingers are still tugging at the flounces on what was supposed to be Zoe's hat, but my gaze suddenly slips down, till I fix on Danny's intense chestnut eyes. I feel his hands rest lightly on either side of my waist and can't believe we're having some kind of... of moment, standing in a wonky stall, surrounded by kids, tractors and the sickly sweet smell of fudge, wearing matching dumb bonnets.

I can't believe it, but I can't remember feeling more thrilled...

Blee-blee-blee-bleep-bleep!!

'Sorry, sorry...' I say, breaking away and scrabbling in my overall pocket for my phone. 'It'll probably be my mum, checking up on me as usual.'

My facing is burning so much that I can't look at Danny. I say my hello while staring at some wilting packets of Marshmallow Swirl fudge on the plate nearest me.

But – amazingly – it wasn't Mum.

'Evie? It's Katie! How's it going?'

'Uh, yeah... busy, but OK,' I say, blushing even more, knowing that Katie would squeal like I'd pinched her if she knew who was standing an arm's-length away from me. 'What about you?'

'Yeah, not bad – been in town all afternoon shopping with my mother.'

'Really?!' I say, not a little bit shocked by the company my best mate's been keeping.

'I know! But her boyfriend just chucked her, so she decided on some retail therapy for herself, and I guess that covers guilt shopping for me too!'

I smile, thinking how pleased Katie sounds, even if she's hiding that behind a sarky remark at her mother's expense.

'But anyway, Evie, I just rang to tell you about this weird call I got this morning...'

'Oh, yeah?' I say, vaguely aware out of the corner of my eye that Danny has pulled off his hat and riffled his hands through his dark straight hair.

'It was from Anita from class; she asked me these really bizarre questions about you, like checking if you were still doing the Steam Rally job today, like you'd mentioned last week at school, and where exactly it was...'

I can't help it, I flip my eyes up and sneak a peek at Danny. He's busy tidying up, gathering paper plates and napkins and hurling them in the bin, while nodding his head in time to some tune he's humming.

'...and so I told her, but when I asked her why,

she said no reason, and made up this excuse about her phone cutting out and she'd have to go. What do you think that was all about?'

'Sorry, Katie – signal's bad here... you're cutting out,' I say, borrowing Danny's sister's little white lie. 'Listen, I'll call you when I get home, OK?'

And with a quick bye, I decide to be brave and ask Danny something.

'Danny?''

'Yep?' He turns from his tidying and smiles.

'All this time you've been helping me here... where's your cousin been?'

Now it's Danny's turn to blush, and I'd put a bet on the fact that he's got elephants trampling around in his belly.

'He... well, I...' he fumbles around for a reason or a fib or something that can get him out of this. But I don't want him to get out of this – I want him to tell me the truth, because I've got a feeling the truth might be delicious...

'Katie said your sister called her,' I tell him, in case that helps ease the truth out of him.

Danny drops his head down to his chest, like a condemned man. But when he raises it back up a few heart-thudding seconds later, he's got a cheeky grin a mile wide on his face.

'My cousin wouldn't come to something like this. My cousin would probably disown me if he knew I'd pretended he was into this steam rally stuff!' he grins. 'I came here 'cause I thought it would be the only way I could maybe get talking to you on your own, without a crowd of girls hovering around you all the time!'

'And, um, what were you going to talk to me about when we were on our own?' I smile, as Danny steps forward and puts his hands around my waist again.

'Well... I might have talked about how much I like you, even when you're dressed like a dental nurse crossed with a milkmaid!'

I'm not sure whether I'm about to hit him or kiss him – but I don't get a chance to do either, 'cause my phone's off again.

'Hi, Mum,' I say, as I watch Danny break away and cheerfully serve a last-minute customer.

'Do I hear a boy's voice there?' her voice cuts in, with that familiar edge of concern.

Ah... I don't really think my mum needs to know that the boy she can hear is my stalker, and I might just be about to start dating him.

'Yeah, that's Danny – he ended up working here today 'cause Mike was short-staffed.'

'Oh, right,' says Mum, her tone instantly relaxing at my explanation.

Normally, I'm pretty good at honesty, but I have told a couple of white lies today.

Still, what I just said to reassure my mum, I realise – as Danny breaks the very last piece of fudge in half and hands it to me – it might just be the the sweetest white lie of all...

Author profile
Sophie Kinsella

It was whilst working as a financial journalist that Sophie wrote her first novel under her real name, Madeleine Wickham. 'The Tennis Party' was immediately hailed a success and she has since published six novels as Madeleine.

However, she is best known as Sophie Kinsella, and for her 'Shopaholic' series of books, selling over a million copies to date.

The latest installment of the Becky Bloomwood story, 'Shopaholic and Sister,' was published in hardback in June 2004.

Problem Page

by Sophie Kinsella

Dear Abby

I really fancy this boy. He works in the bakery shop near where I live in Skegness, and I keep going in to buy things like doughnuts, just so I can look at him. He is *soooo* gorgeous, and has a beautiful smile I can't pluck up courage to speak to him, though. I'm really self-conscious about my figure and always wear baggy T shirts that my Mum says look like dirty dishcloths. What should I do?

Desperate Wendy.

Dear Wendy.

Be brave! The only way to see if you and this boy will hit it off is to talk to him! Remember, he may be ignoring you because he's shy too. Next time you're in the shop, try to strike up a casual conversation.

I'm sure your clothes don't look like dirty dishcloths! Having said that, bright colours can lift your mood and give you confidence. Why not start off with a few bright accessories that make

you feel good?
Good luck!
  Abby

Dear Abby
There's this girl I like. She comes into the shop
where I work and hangs around and I see her
looking at me. She's quiet and shy - and her
clothes look like dirty dishcloths - but I still fancy
her. I don't know what she thinks of me though.
Should I make a move? And what do I say?
  Steve

Dear Steve
Absolutely! Do it!
I feel certain that this girl is coming into your
shop because she's attracted to you. She is
secretly longing for you to talk to her. Next time
you see her, just strike up a casual conversation.
If things seem awkward at first, why not crack a
joke to break the ice?
Good luck!
  Abby

Dear Abby
He spoke to me! But it was really awful.
I went into the shop yesterday and did exactly
what you said. I put on this bright pink scarf, and
big, lime-green sparkly earrings. But he didn't

even notice them. He was just cracking all these awful, tasteless jokes about dead cats in blenders, and looking at me like he expected me to laugh. I think I've gone right off him.

Disappointed Wendy

Dear Abby.

Bloody disaster. She came into the shop yesterday - and I tried to talk to her. All light and jokey, like you said. But she didn't seem to hear a word. She was wearing some stupid psychedelic scarf round her neck that she kept flicking everywhere, and jangling her earrings like a nutter.

I'm giving up on her.

Steve

Dear Wendy

Don't give up! Maybe this boy was trying to impress you with his humour. Perhaps someone even advised him to tell jokes!

Possibly.

Anyway, I think he deserves another chance. I would forget about the brightly-coloured accessories for the moment. Instead, try to get into a proper conversation with him. Really show your personality. You could even disagree with him over something - a friendly argument can often spark things off romantically!

Good luck!
  Abby

Dear Steve
Please don't give up! Maybe this girl was wearing bright colours in order to attract you! I'm having a strong vibe - call it women's intuition! - that she was dressing to impress.

  I'm sure you can still get things going. But I would forget about the jokes for the moment. Instead, why not try to show her that you have a caring side - a love of nature, or animals perhaps. Girls find these qualities very attractive!
  Good luck!
  Abby

Dear Abby
Complete disaster!! I saw him yesterday and did just what you said - but it was terrible! I tried to get the banter going, and start a friendly argument, but it didn't work at all.

  Plus he had this stupid dog there that kept slobbering over all the Danish pastries. It made me feel sick.

  I'm wondering if I even fancy him any more. And I KNOW he doesn't like me. He probably never did.
  Depressed Wendy

Dear Abby

I took your advice. Total nightmare. I took my uncle's puppy in to show how caring I am but she didn't even smile.

In fact, she was a total stroppy cow - disagreed with everything I said. When I said, 'The dog's a dachshund,' she said, 'No he's not, he's a poodle.' She's a psycho. And obviously not interested. I give up.

Steve

Dear Wendy

He likes you!! I know he does!!

OK. Listen. Please, just go in there - no bright accessories, no arguments - and ask if he'd like a coffee sometime. Do this for me, will you?

Abby

Dear Steve

She IS interested!! I know she is!!

OK. Listen. Please, just smile at her next time you see her and say 'How are you?' No jokes. No dogs. Do this for me. Just once. And see what happens.

Abby

Dear Abby

Oh my God! Oh my Goooood! It worked!! We had a coffee together... and he asked me on a date!!

I'm so happy!
Thanx for all your brilliant advice! It really worked!! You're the best agony aunt ever.
Happy Wendy

Dear Abby
Well it worked. I'm seeing her at the weekend. Cheers for all the advice.
Steve.

Dear Wendy
What great news!! I'm so pleased for you. Who would have thought love would blossom over the doughnuts in a bakery shop??!
Abby

Dear Abby
I know. Isn't it lovely?
Blissful Wendy

Dear Steve
What great news!! I'm so pleased for you. Who would have thought love would blossom over the doughnuts in a bakery shop??!
Abby

Dear Abby
Some mistake. I don't work at a bakery shop. I work at a hardware shop, down in Poole.

Cheers for the help, though.

  Steve

Author profile
Stella Duffy

Stella Duffy was born in the UK and grew up in New Zealand. She now lives in London where she works with the comedy company, Spontaneous Combustion, and teaches improvisation to both actors and writers. She has published four short stories and is the author of a play and three novels. Her latest book, 'State of Happiness', was longlisted for The Orange Prize in 2004.

Counting Kisses
by Stella Duffy

I think my mother must have been my first kiss.
Tears and laughing and holding her sides in pain
and kissing me because I was her baby, her first
baby, the only baby she ever thought - in that
moment – that she would want to have. (She
changed her mind later, but fair enough, she was
hurting just then.) My mother's kisses feel gentle,
mostly. They smell like her perfume and her
moisturiser and lamb stew. She works in a shop
where they make lamb stew. It's really good,
quite spicy. But you probably wouldn't want it
every day. And my Mum does wash it off when
she comes home from work, but lamb smell
hangs around. The Japanese can't stand the
smell of cooked lamb. I read that once.

And then my Dad. He didn't stay long, not all
that many kisses I suppose. But seven years
worth. Not bad. Two years to have his kisses to
myself – me and my Mum and then a little
brother to share the kisses. The kisses that came
with his Dad smell – garden and beer and the oil

from the place where he worked. We still see him, every now and then. But his kisses smell different. They smell of another place. And another wife. I don't kiss his other wife. But I do smile. When she's nice. She is the evil stepmother – always will be, no matter how nice she is to me – and God knows she tries – but you can't kiss the evil stepmother. The prince will never come for you if you do. It's the rule. Maybe my Dad just didn't like lamb.

Then there was my little brother. Strictly speaking he didn't kiss me. I kissed him. He sort of mouthed me back, gummed me back, wide-opened his pink lips and showed no teeth. Not yet. I think perhaps you have to have intent for it to be a kiss, not just an open mouth of not-yet-knowing. His baby kisses were really good for the longest time. Mum's milk and baby oil and soft skin kisses. Cradle cap kisses. I didn't mind. Not any of it. Sometimes ammonia-wee kisses. And every now and then just plain old smelly bum kisses. But I always liked them. I liked them because they reminded me that he was little and I was big, because I knew about nappies and washing and changing and feeding, about being a good sister. Because I was such a help to my Mum and my Dad. Such a help to my Mum. I don't kiss my little brother any more. Not since he grew six inches taller than me.

As well as my brother there must have been my Nana and my Grandad, probably my Aunt Sandy and Uncle Bob. My Mum's friend Helen, Dad's brother John. Lots of family kisses. Lots of people whose names I don't remember, or didn't know, and kisses coming together with all the mixed up smells of parties and crisps and beer and wine and perfume and sausage rolls and cake.

I didn't used to like kissing my Nana's Mum, my Great-Gran. I did kiss her - because I liked her - but I didn't like kissing her. She had whiskers, my Nana's Mum. Hard prickly whiskers like an old man. The hair on her head was really thin like an old man's hair too. And she smelled of mint toffees. She always carried mint toffees in her knitting bag. I liked her stories though. About the war and the sound/no-sound of the doodlebugs and the GI she kissed in Piccadilly Circus on VE Day. She was already married by then and she'd had my Nana and my Great-Gran shouldn't have been kissing anyone else at all. Her husband who I never met, because he died years and years ago, he was in Germany and she knew he'd be coming home any day now and she really shouldn't have kissed anyone, not another soul. But she was so happy that the war was nearly over, maybe over, and my Nana was a tiny baby at home and my Great-Gran was out partying with all the girls from her work in Southwark Town Hall. She'd stopped working on the ack-ack guns when she got married. And her husband was away and they were all singing and dancing, so she kissed a GI under the statue of Eros. She never told anyone else about that GI. Just me. I never told anyone else either. When she died my Nana and my Mum went to see her in her coffin. They said I could go if I wanted to. Give her one last kiss. But I didn't want to see her in the coffin. I was scared. My Mum said it was funny, Great-Gran's whiskers were soft on her face, soft since she'd died. I gave my Mum some mint toffees to put in the coffin with her. Just in case.

The next kiss must have been my second year school play. Michael McAllen and he smelled of oranges. Then Lily Narandi. She kissed everyone in the third year on her birthday, said it was what her Mum told her to do. Everyone in the whole class. Well, almost everyone, she didn't kiss Mr Crocker. Don't think Mrs Crocker ever kissed Mr Crocker either. I think the one after that was Andrew Summerskill. We were in the four hundred metres relay team at the sports day and our team won. He kissed me when I crossed the finishing line. He'd passed the baton to Danny

Crasner who gave it to Alison Parker who gave it to me. I was running last because I was our best sprinter. And I crossed the line first and I was laughing and breathing really heavily and my side was hurting so much from the stitch and Andrew Summerskill grabbed me and kissed me because we'd won. Then he kissed Alison Parker and then he kissed Danny Crasner. Alison was upset. She thought Andrew should have kissed her first, not me. She fancied him then. I think she was stupid. I don't think he fancied me or Alison. I'm almost certain he fancied Danny. And he kissed us both so he could kiss Danny too. I'm not sure Danny even noticed. It just looks like the football when England do well and David Beckham kisses Sol Campbell. I reckon that's what Andrew thought anyway. I reckon he thought no one would notice. But I bet he wanted Danny to notice. A little bit anyway.

Then there were some other kisses. A few more parties. And I wasn't so little any more and I got taller as well, though not as tall as my little brother, and I expect I smelled of crisps and beer and wine and perfume. Some kisses I liked and lots I didn't, but I kissed them anyway, was kissed anyway, because that's what you do at parties. What you're supposed to do. If you're lucky. I was usually lucky.

So I haven't counted them all, I couldn't. There must be hundreds, thousands maybe. People I've kissed and kisses that have been given to me. And sometimes I remember them and mostly I don't and lots of them have been the kind of kisses you give because you have to, because your Mum or Dad tell you to, and it would be rude not to. And even more of them have been people I've kissed because I thought they were cute or good-looking or I fancied them one day and wondered the next day how I could ever have fancied them at all and why did I kiss them and I've known that kissing those people with the taste of wine in my mouth is more than half the reason.

And now, there is you. You smell of a perfume or an after-shave I don't know. You smell of a fruit I haven't eaten. You look like the lips I want to kiss. And when I kiss you, you are my first kiss. And maybe my last. I hope you are my last. You are all the kisses added up and everyone else subtracted. Your kisses multiply all the people I have kissed in the past and I know the maths doesn't work, but when I add them together, I end up with just you. Just you and me. No division. We are the sum total. Kiss me. I kiss you.

Author profile
Preethi Nair

Preethi Nair was the one who sat quietly at the back of the class with unstylish centre-parted hair held together by two clips. In a bid to be in with the 'in' crowd, she permed it and placed a green bow at the side. The other kids noticed but not in the way she had hoped. Somewhere between adolescence and thirty, having got rid of the perm, a transformation took place. She now lives in London, has given up trying to set fashion trends and works as a writer.

Her books include 'Gypsy Masala', '100 Shades of White' and 'Beyond Indigo'.

Butterfly
by Preethi Nair

Mr Harris, our biology teacher, shouted above the noise trying to tell us about butterflies.

'The monarch butterfly carries a genetic code that has been passed down through generations. No matter where it is hatched, it can find its way back 2,500 miles to its ancestral origins, to a place it has never been before.'

I'm thinking about the ancestral code handed down from generations through our family - I don't think I'd find my way past Tesco's let alone back to the shores of North India. Not that I come from a dumb family or anything like that, just that my life is home and school, school and home, home and school. It's important to broaden your horizons, that's what I've told my dad hoping he'll understand. I mean he had done it by making the journey from India to England. But unfortunately, his world has shrunk to a terraced house in east London and the furthest he ventures is Ilford (where he works). He won't even let me go to the cinema or on outings because of all those 'Wiseos out there.' Sometimes, I haven't got the energy and can't be bothered to correct him and tell him the word he's looking for is 'weirdos'; it's not because I'm lazy but because sometimes, everything feels like an effort, an uphill sluggish struggle.

'The butterfly is hip.'

Mr Harris managed to stun the class into silence by using the word 'hip'. It's not a word I would have chosen. I would have said butterflies are beautiful but then my class would have pissed themselves laughing.

I wouldn't even begin to compare myself to a butterfly - I'm more of a caterpillar and don't I bloody know it. My nickname at school has just changed to furry - furry Fatima because I'm growing a moustache. Not on purpose, it's just happened - my body seems to be doing it's own thing at the moment, and yeah I'm also called the obvious one - fatty, Fatty Fatima. Am I big? Well if you compare me to Rachel Hopper who's a rake - well then yeah, I suppose I am. It's hard though with a mum who is continually stuffing samosas down you every time she catches sight of you. People talk about East - West cultural difference, arranged marriages blah, blah, blah but do they tell you the main thing? No, they don't. The main difference is in the East, your mum's stuffing samosas down you and if you live in Rachel Hopper's house you get carrots and broccoli.

On a good day, the kids in my class call me funny, 'Funny Fatima'. Don't think I'm funny by nature, more out of necessity. I mean if I wasn't messing about or being funny, I'd be in a corner somewhere, crying my eyes out. It's not like what they say doesn't affect me because inside, it does; but I laugh it off like I couldn't care less.

'After a while, the caterpillars attach themselves head down to a convenient twig, they shed their outer skin and begin the transformation into a pupa (or chrysalis), a process which is completed in a matter of hours.' Mr Harris continued.

Some days, I wish I could have my head down and hang off a stick or a tree trunk or something but that's quite difficult in our house because after homework there are jobs to be done in the house and there can't be no time to sit around and be 'defressed'. That's how my mum says depressed as she can't say her P's - so now I'm thinking maybe she wanted to call me Patima or Patty. Maybe my life would be different had she done this but I'm not going to dwell on this because my life is going to be different.

I'm quite realistic, I know that any transformation that's gonna be taking place in me, isn't gonna happen in a matter of hours. The job's far too big for that so I've got a plan. I shouldn't really admit this but before I go to bed, I turn off the light and in my mind, I imagine I'm a butterfly. I'm free, I don't fit in, I stand out because of the different colours on my wings. I'm beautiful and I can float about doing anything, fly anywhere in the world - it's just my body hasn't made the physical journey with me yet but I know if I focus hard enough on making the transformation in my mind - one day, I know it will.

'Fatima Palek. Are you listening? Pay attention, Fatima. Stop wasting time daydreaming. It will get you nowhere.' Mr Harris shouted.

'I'm dreaming of crossing frontiers, of making a journey Mr Harris.'

The class roared out laughing.

'The only journey you'll be making is to Mr Mitchell's office.' He replied.

'No, it won't be.' I answered back, not meaning to offend Mr Harris but just voicing the thoughts in my head.

'I'll have none of your cheek, Fatima Palek. Get down to Mr Mitchell's office now and tell him why I have sent you.' Mr Harris shouted.

So I went to Mr Mitchell's office and told him why I had been sent 'for using my imagination, for crossing frontiers,' I said. And instead of Mr Mitchell shouting at me and giving me detention and that, he suggested going to Mrs Pope's art club after school so I could 'put my imagination to better use.' I told him my dad wouldn't let me but

Mr Mitchell said he would call him and have a word.

My dad has never had a Headmaster call him and tell him that he had a talented kid and he was flattered also he didn't think there would be any 'Wiseos' in Mrs Pope's art club so he let me go.

The first day there, I absolutely loved it and began by painting butterflies so I could experiment with colours. Then I painted the person I would be and the things I would do, I painted places I would visit and Mrs Pope was dead impressed and she said, there were no two ways about it, I had talent and would go far. If Mrs Pope said that and she knew what she was talking about then maybe I would. Maybe that's all we need - someone to help us believe.

Fifteen years later, Fatima Palek made the transformation and has become an award winning artist. She is commissioned to paint pictures all over the world. Like the butterfly which inspired her, Fatima travelled over 2,500 miles and visited the place where her father was from and somewhere deep inside of her, it felt like it was a journey she was always destined to make.

Author profile
Cathy Hopkins

Cathy Hopkins lives in North London with her handsome husband and three deranged cats. Or is it the other way around?

She has sold nearly a million copies of her books to date and has had over twenty titles published.These include the eight titles in the 'Mates, Dates' series, and the four in the 'Truth, Dare, Kiss or Promise' series. The ninth title in the 'Mates Dates' series, 'Mates, Dates & Great Escapes', was published in August 2004.

An extract from

Mates, Dates and Cosmic Kisses

by Cathy Hopkins

'Shall we go and have a walk before we go home?' asked Mark.

I felt really nervous. It was our first date. Would he want to kiss me? I've only ever kissed two other boys and neither of them were important. One boy when I was a kid and then some creepoid last year who had a nasty case of wandering hands. It was horrible and he poked his tongue in my mouth. All I could think was wet fish. Sloppy, slimey. Blaghh.

This time it would be for real.

I tried to remember what Nesta's brother has told us about kissing. Tony fancies himself as the Master Snogger and one time, before he was going out with Lucy, he even offered to show me how it was done. I laughed at him but now I wished I'd taken him up on it. I mean, how do you know if you're a good kisser? I cast my mind back and desperately tried to remember what his snogging tips were. I should have asked Lucy or Nesta before I came out. I know I thought, I'll phone them.

'Sure, a walk sounds good,' I said. 'But just got to go to the ladies. Won't be a mo.'

I dashed into the ladies, waited until all the cubicles were empty then dialled Lucy's number.

'Lucy,' I said. 'I'm with Mark. What do I do if he tries to kiss me?'

Lucy laughed. 'D'oh. Snog him back, dummy.'

'But how?' I wailed. 'I'm really worried I'll be useless at it and he'll never want to see me again.'

'Relax,' said Lucy. 'Just take your lead from him.'

'What if he puts his tongue in my mouth? What do I do?'

'Just do what feels natural,' said Lucy

'Thanks,' I said feeling none the wiser. I phoned Nesta for a second opinion.

'Fresh breath,' she said. 'V. important. Otherwise keep the pressure varied. Soft, medium, hard and run your fingers through his hair. Boys like that.'

'What do I do with my tongue?'

'Stick it up his nostril,' she giggled.

'Ergh, Nesta!'

'Izzie, relax. You'll be fine. Ring me later with the details.'

Thanks for nothing Nesta, I thought as I switched off my phone. Just because she's snogged loads of boys she thinks it's really funny.

I checked my appearance in the mirror. Luckily my hair has gone back to its natural chestnut colour and the green dye that I put in for my step sister's wedding had pretty well gone. I rooted round in my bag and found some chewing gum then put on some lipstick. Oh. Was that a good idea? If he kisses me he'll get it all over him. Maybe I should wipe it off again? God, it's so complicated. We ought to have lessons in this sort of thing at school instead of all that stuff we never need about how many crops are grown in some remote country I've never heard of.

I rubbed my lipstick into my lips so that it wasn't too shiny, then went back out to meet him. Gulp! He was chewing gum as well. Snogging was definitely on the cards. I pushed my gum behind my teeth so he wouldn't see that I was chewing too. I didn't want him to think I was expecting it or anything.

When we got outside, we mooched about for a bit and had a look at what was on at the movies then it started raining so we made a dash for the bus-stop. We were the only people there and I wondered if he was going to make a move. Or should I? Did he need to know I wanted him to kiss me? Or would that seem forward?
I tried to do a come on look like I've seen in romantic films but I think I looked more like a grinning hyena than a femme fatale. And I was

shivering like mad though I wasn't sure if that was from the cold or nerves.

After agonising for two minutes, Mark stepped forward and put his arms around me. He felt gorgeous. Warm, solid and safe.

'Freezing, isn't it?' he said. 'Let's keep each other warm.'

I went rigid. This is it, I thought. Get ready to pucker.

He leant his face towards me and I moved towards him and we banged noses.

'Oops,' he laughed. Then he leant in again and kissed me.

At first it was a shock feeling his soft lips on mine and all I could think was what to do with my hands? Run your fingers through his hair, I thought, remembering Nesta's advice. I reached up to the back of his head but my fingers got stuck. Gel. His hair was like glue. Oh no. And I still had my gum in my mouth. Gulp. I swallowed it.

Then I wondered what he'd done with his. He wasn't chewing anymore. Then I got an attack of the giggles.

'What are you laughing at?' he said looking taken aback.

'Er, I...just swallowed my gum.'

He looked mischievously. 'So did I.'

Then he stared at my mouth and a thrill of

anticipation ran through me. It's the strangest feeling in the world, like a sweet pain but just lovely.

'Come here.' He said pulling me close to him again and putting my arms around his waist. Then he kissed me properly. A lovely soft deep kiss and this time our noses didn't bang. It felt perfect. Cosmic. And I wanted it to go on forever.

'You're a good kisser,' he said pulling back after a few minutes.

'Thanks,' I said, thinking yippee, I'm a natural. Then I kissed him again. Practice makes perfect. That's going to be my new motto.

Author profile
Matt Whyman

As well as fast gaining a reputation for himself
as an innovative and exciting author of teenage
novels, Matt is the regular advice columnist for
Bliss magazine, as well as on-line adviser for aol
and has made frequent guest appearances on TV,
radio and the internet. As well as 'Superhuman'
and his advice books for young people, 'XY' and
'XY100', Matt is also the author of the young adult
novel, 'Boy Kills Man', which is fast gaining
critical acclaim. He is currently working on his
next young adult novel, 'The Wild,' which will be
published in July 2005.

Superhuman
by Matt Whyman

An incoming squeal floods into the station, like
the brakes on a runaway train. Pigeons flock to
the crossbeams. They squabble for a perch in the
vaults overhead, but fail to settle as the volume
builds. Had anyone been present this time of
night, they might wheel around in horror – only
to find the tracks are lifeless, the platforms
deserted and the ticket kiosks closed. No trains
run until dawn but, make no mistake, an unseen
force is closing in and fast. A shadow drops into
the mix next, right there on the polished marble
floor. It pools at the foot of a covered escalator –
and that's when all hell comes flooding out.

First a figure launches from the lip of the
handrail, sparking an end to that terrible sound.
He's crouched on a skateboard, early teens
perhaps, his arms flung outwards as he arcs into
the air. The momentum from his noisy grind to
ground level propels the board some distance,
but he's not doing this for show. That becomes
apparent when the wheels connect with the floor
and a dozen or so figures flock from the escalator

mouth like bats out of a cave.

'C'mon! He's ours!'

These guys are a little older, and a whole lot meaner looking. They move by rollerblade, their leather trench coats flapping noisily as they spread out after their quarry. Still he moves with a god-given grace, our boy with the board, his wheels barely touching the floor. A kick flip takes him high over a bench, buying precious seconds as the swiftest skaters are forced to swarm around it. The rearguard goon attempts to mimic his move, only to clip the bench and fall in a sprawling heap. The collision distracts the rest of the gang, who turn to scowl and curse just a beat too long.

For when they switch back around the boy has vanished, and all they can do is glance at one another as if perhaps they have just been fooled by a ghost.

There was a time when the station opened twenty-four hours a day, but as the city became dangerously unsafe after dark, it made sense to close it down at night. Nobody travelled far from home after daylight, after all. Not if you wanted to reach your destination with your wallet in your pocket or your heart still beating. By rights the security guards should've been here, but everyone knew they skulked home soon after locking up the last exit. They valued their own safety, after all.

Which was why the boy had headed for the guards' office, just behind the trolley storage – the office with the unmarked door and all the monitors inside. A place where he could hide.

On the screens, he has six different views of the station's interior, and that's how he can see the pack circling. They stalk the cathedral-like space in silence, rolling this way and that. He thinks of vultures waiting for their prey to let go of all hope, and tries not to breathe in case they hear him. His heart works like a jackhammer, but he can't afford to swallow, or even drop a bead of sweat. If they sniff him out it'll all be over. He might see the sun rise over the city but it won't be the same. Whatever punishment these guys choose to deliver, he knows it'll surely spell the end to his skating days, and he really doesn't need that now. Not when he's starting to find his feet.

With his board in one hand, and his back pressed to the door, he watches the monitors and waits. It's all he can do. The night is on the cusp of lifting, and if he can hold out just a little longer this crew will retreat to the other half of the city. They'll have to for this chase started way out West from here, on their turf. Unlucky for them that the station lies on his side of the boundary line, but it just might be the break he badly needs. For the long leather coats and the blades they wear mark them out as enemy. It's the badge over there, but not here in the East. This is his territory, where anything goes so long as you're on a skateboard.

He knows that if they're spotted word will quickly spread, which is why they look so wary as they continue to hunt him down.

So he waits and he worries for his crew . . .

Crash and Spinner had been some way behind when the ambush kicked off. It was just typical for these two to hang back in the subway sidings, getting up the finest colours that they could on all the railcars. The next morning, oh man, the city would see their pieces when the trains pulled through the platforms. A moving art gallery, that's how they saw it. When it came to graffiti, these guys were king, even if they had to travel far to keep their crown.

The entire crew was way out West at the time, and by rights they should've stuck together. The big guy, Marvin, and his cousin, Tiny Ti, had insisted on creeping even deeper into the network of tunnels, just to bomb the brickwork with their own ink. Enemy territory went down to the clay in this city, and at the time they were right underneath the boulevards and boutiques that made the West what it was: a place for the wealthy, with no room or time for anyone else less fortunate. That's what had started this whole conflict, long before they were born, and that's why this crew had pretty much grown up with graffiti in their blood. Marking territory like this was a way of life. Unless you staked your claim then you were nothing, and being noticed in the right way is crucial to our boy on the board – especially when it comes to the last member of this band of board-disciples.

He had taken on the rollerbladers for Katya's sake. One minute the pair of them had been whispering about how they'd like to see the suckers' faces when they found this kind of calling card, the next the suckers themselves had come out of the shadows, with all eyes on the girl. It explained why he acted on instinct, snapping his board to hand and charging for the weakest-looking weed on wheels. It had worked, as well: the geek went down with one swing of his deck. Enraged and baying for blood, the others had promptly abandoned Kat to hunt him down.

Panic had threatened to overtake him from that moment on, but his flight instinct held true and delivered him here – to the relative safety of the monitoring room. He can barely believe he's made it right now, but it will make sense some day. Minutes earlier, down in the subway network,

217

he had commanded every muscle in his body to deliver him home. Sprinting was never his first choice when it came to making a mistake, but on that broken surface his board would have needed wings as well as wheels. The ballast bed had granted the bladers an advantage, for they could straddle the rails. As he tore through the half darkness he had heard them closing in behind, the rumble of their wheels on the steel both steady and true. All he could do was hope and pray that the next station would soon reveal itself. Had that circle of light not appeared around a bend in the tunnel, they would surely have mown him down.

He had followed his board up on to the subway platform, slamming it there like a surfer attempting to catch a wave and landing on it belly up. Within seconds he was upright again and moving as he knew best. From there, it had been a question of speeding through the labyrinth of linked tunnels and inspection routes, even riding the roof of an eastbound freight train: anything to surface at the City Railroad Station as if his life depended on it.

Now, from his hiding place in the guards' office, he scans the banks of monitors and dares to think he might be safe. Each screen feeds a different take on the hunt going on outside the

218

door. He almost laughs when he thinks about it, but giving away his location just wouldn't be funny so he settles for a private smile. With every angle of the station concourse covered, he can see the rollerbladers have regrouped at the foot of the covered escalator. They could be a hockey team at half time, he thinks, watching them form a circle and then revolve as one as they discuss the next option. He sees a lot of shaking heads, and can hear them cursing his name, but that's fine by him. They'll be gone within minutes and he'll be free to catch up with Katya and the rest of his crew. Unless, that is, one of them attempts to make contact with him first.

When his mobile phone begins to sing, his first response is to claw at the knapsack as if it's scalding the small of his back. He finds the phone in amongst all his spray paints, but he doesn't shut it down. It's too late for that now. Instead, he takes the call and looks on in terror at the scene unfolding on the monitors.

'Hullo?' His voice squeaks a little, but he's too freaked out to clear his throat and try again.

'Well, that went well.' The boy recognises her dry, deadpan voice immediately, and the receiver burns against his ear. Even if that's the last voice he hears before he falls to the crew now gliding ominously towards his hideaway, at least he can face them with Katya here in spirit.

'Are you OK?' she asks him, softening now.

'Everyone else is fine, we're almost home, but what's your position?'

A knock at the door follows, as if to punctuate Kat's question. He frowns at the screen, for he had expected the gang to kick it open on hearing his mobile ring out. Despite feeling sick to the core, he asks her to hold on. When he opens up they're waiting for him, united by their smug grins which only rich kids from the West can muster.

'What's my position?' he repeats into the mouthpiece, his eyes locked on the ringleader.

'Not good.'

The rollerbladers begin to chuckle at this grim understatement, only to be silenced by a background squeal – the second to spill into the station in one night. They react as a pack: swivelling around smartly as if that runaway train really is coming this time. Then another shadow pools at the foot of the covered escalator, followed by three, four, five kids on skateboards. All of them recover quickly from the leap, and reform in a defiant line. This lot are dressed in radical colours: a ripped-up street punk look just like the lad whose skin they've come to save.

They might be kind of young and scrawny looking, but there's a huge guy with them, in a T-shirt that reads: whale. He's built like a tank on top, with short-cropped hair like he's destined for a life in the military. His shoulders are so broad, in fact, that he's able to support a boom box on one side. The way he has it pinned there with one paw, you'd think it was a permanent feature. The other two lads don't look up too much, but the spray cans holstered on their belts confirm a unique kind of quick-draw. A couple of girls are with them, too. The really small one has her hair pulled into giant pigtails and a vicious sneer on her face. The girl beside her is dressed as if she only comes alive at night, all in black, with raven hair and pale white skin, yet she too appears to be relishing this moment. She cups her elbow in one palm, presses a phone to her ear, and winks at the boy behind the luckless rollerbladers. This is Katya, of course.

'Lucky for you the cavalry's here,' she says. 'What would you do without us?'

He is about to protest that he could've handled this alone - but it's too late for that now. The two sides are squaring up already.

'Yo!' The big guy with the buzz cut and the extra large T-shirt doesn't move when he speaks to these guys, not a single twitch. His voice seems slowed down, too, but it's certainly deep enough to command their attention. 'We can have this out, right here and now, but whatever goes down you'll never make it home.' He gestures to the station's glass frontage, at the brightening strip of sky below the stairs. Dawn is creeping up at the corner of this city now, which is the last thing the rollerbladers need so far from home. 'The East is waking up, man. Always does get the sunshine first, which means anytime now the bigger boys are gonna rise and wonder what the bad smell is coming outta here.'

The bladers glance at one another, looking pumped still but increasingly nervous. Behind them, our boy with the board clips out of the room, circling wide to join his crew. He is met by a furious stare from the ringleader opposite, but responds in kind as best he can. For a moment, nobody moves. It's all in the looks these two are dealing each other. The boy is clearly on edge, and blinks despite himself. For the ringleader, this is all he needs to see. He pushes back his greasy blonde hair, smiling to himself. Next he lifts his fist and jabs a thumb westward. He's the first to roll as well, never letting his gaze drop as he retreats towards the glass doors. The others follow stopping only when their main man draws out a canister from the inside pocket of his trenchcoat. He shakes it briefly, tests the paint in the air, and then turns to the glass again. With his back to the skateboarders, he pumps out four slashes of black paint, but even before he steps away they know he's leaving behind his crew's trademark 'W'.

'Our card,' he says, and performs a mock bow. 'In case you've forgotten just who you're messing with here.'

'Ooh, scary.' This from the shorter of the two girls, the one with the outsized pigtails and the attitude. Tiny Ti, she's called and nobody has ever needed to ask why. She blows them all a kiss goodbye, and then her face opens out in surprise. 'Look out, guys, behind you!'

The bladers whip around, two of them turning right into each other. They go down like clowns on banana skins, but it's egg that's left all over their faces when they find that they've been scammed. For all they find behind them are their own reflections in the glass.

The ringleader turns to glare at the girl. He's lost for words but his expression says it all.

'Made you look,' she says with a shrug. 'One more thing, perhaps you could leave some money for all the damage you've caused?'

'It's paint,' he says. 'Leave it to the cleaners. This kind of thing keeps your people in jobs.'

'Fun-nee,' she says icily. 'I was thinking of all the glass that'll need replacing.'

The ringleader studies the fresh tag as if he's missing something. 'Why?' he asks eventually.

She presses a finger to her chin. 'Duh – it's

locked?' She waits for him to test the doors for himself. 'Now drop a couple of notes in the charity box over there, and leave in an orderly fashion.'

Even as she speaks, his face is turning crimson: a mixture of shame and rage. He debates the deal with himself, then gives a nod to his right-hand man. This guy can't believe what he's been instructed to do, but a kick to the shin soon persuades him to go fold some money into the box. Our boy with the board? He glances along his own crew, still lined up in a show of strength, and shares a look with the girl at the other end. The graffiti war will never be over but they can claim this particular conflict, one that finishes with the sound of crashing glass.

The ringleader leads the way, having built up the necessary speed by describing an arc across the marble like some kind of demon speed skater. The others follow close behind, unfolding in a spiral before snaking out into the slate grey light. The city is on the verge of awaking, first the East and then the West.

For Katya, Crash and Spinner, Big Marvin and Tiny Ti, it's the end of another long Friday night. For Jude Ash, the boy whose wheels have barely touched the ground, who comes alive on a board in a way that startles even him, this is only the beginning . . .

The Judges

Meg Cabot
Author

Helen Johnston
Bliss Editor

Meera Syal
Comedienne and author

George Grey
Waterstone's Children's Manager

Caroline Roby and Lucy Allan
Hollyoaks scriptwriters

Introduction

by Meg Cabot

To celebrate World Book Day on 4th March 2004, Bliss Magazine, in conjunction with Waterstone's, set its readers a challenge to write a short story under one of four categories; 'The Kiss', 'The Phone Call', 'The Scream' and 'The Journey'.

The aim was to unveil Britain's hottest young writing talent, and to give them a chance to see their work in print.

The competition has been huge success and we have been overwhelmed by the response, receiving more than 6000 entries.

After much deliberation my fellow judges and I chose four category winners and one over-all winner. Here are the results....

Category winner & overall winner

Teen Writing Competition 2004
in association with Waterstone's & Bliss magazine

Anna Burnell
Aged 16, from Sheffield

What inspired your story?
'It's inspired by an actual school trip to London, one of my teachers and certain people in my school. All sort of blended together to make them more entertaining, but all based on truth too.'

Who's your favourite author and why?
'J.R.R. Tolkien. I have read absolutely everything he's written and love it all, he's so imaginative and convincing. I know my story is very modern and real, but I really enjoy reading fantasy.'

What does winning mean to you?
'Everything, this is so exciting, thank you. I've always wanted to be a writer and this has encouraged me so much.'

The Journey
by Anna Burnell

I have rebellious toes. A slightly odd observation,
I know, but I've been sat on this train for two
hours now and trust me, my feet are all I have
left to look at. How long does it take to get to
London anyway? I put my name down for this
History trip to the Public Records Office to get a
day off school, and maybe squeeze a little
shopping in after the visit. Only I got informed by
Mr '1066' Smedley that the visit will take all day.
That's if we ever get there. I've been sat behind
my history teacher, Smelly Smedley for an hour
now, and I can't help thinking that he looks more
like my little brother's iguana every minute. His
eyes keep swivelling about unnervingly. I wonder
if he can see me. Hope not, seeing as I've been
painting lip gloss lips on his reflection in my
window. One has to keep oneself entertained in
these monotonous situations. I'll tell you
something though. He's a tad freaky, t'old Smed.
He's one of those guys that is just like your
average boring tweed-clad history teacher, with a
red nose and piper's cough, but he has this 'cool-

gone-wrong' side to him too. He wears lime green socks, for God's sake. I've been idly captivated by them for twenty minutes. He is one of those unfortunate people who has a bald patch and yet still has dandruff.

Great, here comes Malcolm. He's the only one on this trip who's actually interested in History. He must be the secret spawn of Smed. Thing is, he has an interest in me too. In fact, lucky me, he's sitting down next to me! Why do his legs have to take up so much room? He's like an overgrown stick insect. The 'conversation' goes as follows:

Malcolm: 'Tell me, Natalie, why is it that you are all on your lonesome?'

Me: 'Because I've been wise enough to distance myself from the likes of you, dear Malc. Where's Wet Linda with her wooden leg anyway? I thought she was the love of your pathetic little life?'

Malcolm: 'I broke it off. Get it? Broke it off.' This is followed by a sort of goat-with-diabetes laugh from this idiot. He is obviously quite destitute of any sanity.

At this point I am approached by an eager looking bloke in a grubby parka, who asks me to give up my seat. The cheek of it. Decide to give in for the sake of escaping Malcolm, and anyway this guy could be one of those freaky Psychology students studying Obedience. And I wouldn't want to be an anomaly in his results after all. Who knows what strange skills these psychology swots have. I shuffle past a still snorting Malcolm, reminding him that his freckles could be cancerous, and end up next to a snorting Chinese bloke on the opposite side of the carriage. I entertain myself for a while by observing the sheep whizzing by. Why is it that sheep don't shrink in the rain?

I reach across the recumbent figure next to me in order to purchase a coffee from the passing trolley. I blow on it noisily, but the guy just snores louder. Obviously he was as bored as me. He's beginning to dribble. I would lend the guy a tissue but my boredom prevents me from doing so, and instead I end up watching the saliva work its way down the guy's chin. Will it make it to his chest? It's a close call, but YES! It's down, and making its way into his collar... oh no. I have just tipped half my coffee down this bloke's neck. Oh God. I have scalded a man. He'll be scarred for life. I stare at him for a while, but he doesn't even move. Oh God. What if he's dead? What if he died in his sleep and I poured coffee on to a corpse? A corpse with scald marks. I don't like dead things; they're not natural. Wait- he's still snoring. Phew! I sink down into my seat in relief as a polished female voice comes over the tannoy:

  'Next stop, Crawley, Thank you.'

Why are these voices always so fake? Do you
have to go to some sort of school of cheesiness
to qualify for that job? Or are they just voices?
Voices with no bodies…. I started practising my
most superficial voice… 'Hello, I am a fake bimbo,
the next stop is Glasgow.' At that moment I jump
out of my skin as the Chinese guy leaps up, cries
'My stop!' And runs off down the carriage. I
wouldn't mind but we're going to London.

  On gazing into the aisle in complete
befuddlement, I notice that he's gone and left his
bag behind. But wait? What if he meant to? What
if… what if, it's a bomb? What if we all explode,
right here on the most boring trip ever? I'll never
get to marry Orlando Bloom. I'll never get to be a
famous writer and hang out in swanky bars. Wait
Natz, I tell myself. (Yes I admit that I have a
slight problem with talking to myself, but going
mad doesn't matter when you're going to die.) I
should tell t'old Smed. He knows all about
bombs, being a war boff. He was probably in
World War One. He'll know what to do. I shuffle
cautiously to the edge of my seat so that I don't
accidentally attract the attention of Malcolm. I
don't want to have to spend my last minutes with
him snorting down my ear. I lean across to Smed
in order to whisper to him our current

predicament, only to find him deeply engrossed in the 'Dear Deidre' problem pages in the paper. What is he thinking? I wriggle back into my seat in disgust. The bomb can wait. Never mind History. Seems to me that old Smed needs a proper education...

Category Winner
The Kiss

Gemma Taylor
Aged 16, from Birmingham

What inspired your story?
'It may sound like I'm making this up but reading Meg Cabot's stories for so long have been a massive inspiration to me. I like her style and I really tried to imitate this in 'The Kiss.'

Who's your favourite author and why?
'Meg Cabot. I think she's a very funny writer, her books are really easy to read and they're really entertaining.'

What does winning mean to you?
'It's made me think that I could possibly go into writing as a career, it's opened up another pathway for me. It means so much to me to win this, I'm thrilled!'

First Choice
by Gemma Taylor

OK so I suppose I should kind of do an introduction or something into my life. My name is Alex, well it's actually Alexandra but nobody ever calls me that. I am sixteen and have never been kissed which I know is totally sad. Although if I was a guy I wouldn't go near me either. Basically I am over weight, tall so I'm like the BFG and I have frizzy ginger hair. Oh yeah and totally enormous out of control breasts. And to top it all off my best friend Nat is ultra skinny and has long straight platinum blond hair.

Nat is a really great friend she just has one flaw and that is that she is totally in love with my older brother Ollie who is eighteen and is in a band called 'The Juveniles'. There are four other members James, Rick, Matt and Josh, all of whom are totally fit and have seen me playing with my Barbie doll in the bath naked!

My top three New Year's resolutions:
1. Get fit and lose weight.
2. Get a boyfriend.
3. Always cleanse tone and moisturise.

Me and Nat decided to do a kickboxing class to get fit, and to check out the ultra gorge boys. However I almost died just doing the warm up which consisted of about a zillion sit ups and press ups. We also had to run, a two mile run in fact.

'Now girls we're going for a short run, you are welcome to join us, but we would hate for you to break a nail or anything.' The weird coach had kindly informed us.

See how he practically bullied us into doing it!

We both managed to finish the run which was a track through a wood, but we did arrive about half an hour after everyone else. But still what do you expect when you haven't done exercise since, well let's face it never. Oh yeah and your huge breasts are flying about everywhere. It was a wonder I didn't knock myself out.

Everyone else was already stretching and getting their breath back.

'Well, well, well, I thought I'd have to send some of my lads out to search for you two,' he laughed heartily at his own joke. Yeah really bloody funny at least we finished it.

Then I passed out in front of everyone and when I came round I found myself on top of a really cute guy with my boobs in his face. I was helped up by other guys who led me inside to sit down. One of them kept his arm round me which

I thought was really sweet. They were really cute and I could see their huge muscles.

'Hi I'm David and he's Graham.'

'I'm Nat and that's Alex,' she said pointing at me.

We reached the bench and I sat down feeling extremely stupid. Graham passed me his water bottle, Graham was the cute guy that had his arm around me.

'Here have some of this,' he said smiling at me as he passed me the water; I noticed that he had dark brown eyes like a never ending tunnel.

I smiled gratefully that they were being so nice.

'Why do you think you passed out?' David asked.

Nat butted in before I could say anything.

'Well she hasn't had anything to eat all day,' she said.

I almost choked as I shot her an evil look. David and Graham looked at me.

'Why not?' Graham asked.

'She thinks she's fat and is going on some mad diet thing,' said Nat.

If they didn't think I was strange then they sure do now, thanks a bunch Nat. I mean hello I may have just passed out but it has not affected my speech. I hadn't done it on purpose. I had got up late for school and practically ran the whole way there and then I had detention. I told them all this but no one looked convinced.

'You are so not fat Alex,' Graham said. I kind of nodded, too angry to speak. It was quite sweet of him to say that but I know that he is only lying to be nice to me.

'Right well I'll drop you both off home after the lesson to make sure you get home ok,' David said.

'Thanks,' said Nat now flirting with him.

David drove us home, with Nat in the front with him; me and Graham were in the back. David put on some really loud rock music so we couldn't really talk much; Nat had other things in mind though.

It was really dark by the time we pulled up to my house and Nat was all over David. Graham had put his arm around me when we had got into the car, so we were sitting really close. Watching Nat kissing David I felt really awkward in case Graham tried to do that to me, and I know that it would be really great and all but I didn't want to mess things up with a really cute guy that I only just met. Anyway as I was worrying he leant over, I quickly debated giving him the cheek but this would be my first real kiss, so I let him carry on and I'm telling you that there's nothing to it and it felt great. We could have sat there all night for all I cared but Nat and David were messing around and knocked the off button on the radio, but still I suppose we couldn't have stayed there all night. We kissed goodbye and exchanged phone numbers before we headed in.

'So did you really mean it when you said I wasn't fat?' I asked.

'Of course I meant it. Look at you, you're gorgeous.' Graham is so sweet, I think I'm in love and I have had my first real kiss. Life is just perfect.

Category Winner
The Phone Call

Ploy Radford
Aged 14, from Suffolk

What inspired your story?
'I love history and so decided to write a book set in the future. Also English is one of my favourite subjects and I love writing so it seemed a good idea to blend the two.'
Who's your favourite author and why?
'Philippa Gregory because she writes stuff set in Tudor times and they're really historical books.'
What does winning mean to you?
'It hasn't sunk in yet! It's given me confidence that I can actually write and it's made my ambition of being a journalist seem easier to achieve.'

The Phone Call
by Ploy Radford

She impatiently dragged her mother into the cool, modern interior of the mobile phone shop, her eyes already roaming over the many different models displayed on the wall. She took no notice of which ones were cheaper or offered the better deals, she was intent on hunting for the model all her friends had been raving about.

'Can I have this one - please mummy?' she wheedled.

Her mother rolled her eyes at the smartly dressed assistant with slick hair and a well-practiced smile who moved towards them.

Tarn Makler saw it, a single gleam of silver amongst the rubble of the abandoned brick buildings of Old London. He reached forward, gently brushed the dust away and carefully placed the mobile in a container. He excitedly signalled his find to his fellow archaeologists, unable to speak due to the cover of his face, designed to keep the pollution, from being this close to the ground, out.

Now she had a mobile phone she was always texting. She had become so fast at it that her father joked that her thumb would become bigger and musclier than the rest of her. She would ignore him with a dignified air as she continued texting her friends.

Tarn gently thumbed the well-worn keypad, as he sat in his laboratory on the top levels of the New British History Museum. The finding of this model of mobile still in working condition was very rare. Artefact, no. 11675 would be a welcome addition to the museum. He entered 'messages' then 'inbox' and began reading the texts in there.

'Guess wot? James and I r now a couple! :) Asked me out after my b-day party. Wot a gr8 way to turn 15! Cu l8er luv Izzy'

Tarn shook his head. How times had changed; in this day and age there were laws banning intimate contact amongst minors, even kissing. The era the former owner of this mobile was from was often referred to as the 'easy' era amongst historians. He personally felt the moral decline was often exaggerated but the contrast between that time and now was sharp.

'I h8 teachers so much :(Wish they wud get off my case. Dnt care bout hmwk. Tb luv May'

Tarn smiled wryly. 'Some things never change' he thought. Tarn had hated school. He had hated being stuck in the same classroom all day in front of the same computer. The incessant humming was annoying, as was losing your work when the class bully decided to pull the plug out of your computer. Sport hadn't been much better, he had gone to a local comprehensive, only private schools were based in the countryside where you could play outside on real grass; grass didn't survive long in London anymore.

Tarn rubbed his tired blue eyes. He was going to have a word with the caretaker to see if he could get better sunlight replicator lamps, the harsh light from the current ones were giving him a headache. It was midday though; the caretaker would be on his lunch break.

Photo messaging was the most entertaining form of communication. The funnier, grosser or more daring the picture taken, the better. Bored boys took pictures of themselves attempting stupid stunts or just doing disgusting things and sent them to girls in a hope to impress them. The girls didn't like being outdone.

Tarn openly chuckled as he scrolled through the photos. The first one was a picture of a dark looking kid being bitten by one of the pelicans in St. James's Park. The only pelicans left in Britain now were the stuffed ones in the

Natural History Museum.

The next picture was obviously sent in a bid to impress the mobile's owner; it showed a guy launching through the air on a skateboard. From the blurred pixels he could determine the boy was handsome and healthy. Tarn glanced up at his reflection in the window. He was considered handsome but not in a healthy way. The English climate was against him, as was his purse.

Actually phoning someone wasn't really done, unless it was necessary for a lift home or something; the phone rates just seemed to eat away at the credit. She always kept her phone on though so she could reply to messages immediately and perhaps even receive a phone call from Ash. He had asked for her phone number the other night when they were hanging around the fish and chip shop after school.

Tarn keyed in the voicemail service number with growing anticipation; if it was rare to find mobile phones of this make, it was even rarer to find one that had a voice message still in its memory. After a pause a mechanical female's voice without an ounce of emotion in it spoke announcing that there was one new message. Tarn gave a whoop, attracting the attention of his colleagues who came over to his work area. Tarn carried on listening to the rest of the message. The mechanical voice was replaced by a chirpy one accompanied by background noise.

'Hi darling it's mum. Can you do me a huge favour sweetie and buy some tissues, oh and some onions, Theresa's coming over for tea and I want to cook her that French dish your little ahem guy friend's mum showed me, bye.'

'The boss is going to love you 'ssociate,' exclaimed Drewser, clapping Tarn on the back, 'the accent and use of language is beautiful.'

She now had a part time job and could afford the new model. She carelessly offered it to her little brother. He didn't want 'the ancient thing', so he left it in the basement.

The mobile phone was set up in a little exhibit all of its own, in the museum, with the message being replayed every fifteen minutes.

Category Winner
The Scream

Jasmine Robinson
Aged 16, from Norfolk

Jasmine is a prolific writer and entered for three of the four categories in the competition. But it was her story, 'Blanche', that really impressed the judges the most. The story shows the relationship between a young boy and a wild Camargue horse violently cut short. It symbolises everything that has been lost and a bond that has been broken between the animal and the boy.

Blanche
by Jasmine Robinson

It was dawn in the marshes of the Camargue.
It was midsummer and already warm, despite the
early hour. The water still, only the briefest ripple
pierced its glacial surface as a dragonfly darted
across. Suddenly a thundering of hooves
shattered the quiet as a herd of white Camargue
horses galloped down the track. The dragonfly
soared upwards and watched the dirt sprayed up
as the sharp hooves of the horses dug the soil
and as a cloud of dust rose and was illuminated
by the sun slowly rising in the sky. The still air
was filled with frenzied equine shrieks and shrill
whinnies as the horses galloped.

A human whoop broke the air. Following the
herd was Quentin, standing high in his stirrups
above the back of his own grey mare. With his
stick in the air he yelled at the herd and drove
them forward. His face was glowing like a beacon
with excitement and adrenaline. A sudden breeze
whipped his light brown hair and his rabbit-like
eyes took in the slightest disturbance in the pace
of the herd. To his left rode Thibaut, on his grey

247

mare, Anne-Marie. He did not ride as hard as Quentin, his stick hung loosely by his side and he urged on the animals with encouraging noises.

The dragonfly watched the chaotic rabble of sweating horseflesh pass and as the dust settled back to the ground the marshes were still again.

As time passed the mad stampede slowed to a canter, then a sloping, awkward trot and finally relaxed down to a walk. They had a distance to travel, and some of the older mares were tiring. The boss mare, named 'The Beast' by Quentin (due to her bullying nature), had slowed considerably. She was getting on in years, but she was still very much respected by the rest of the herd and they followed behind, happy for her to set the pace.

However, a yearling filly was getting skittish and excitable. She barged in front, head in the air and squealing as if she was being tortured. The Beast gave a shriek of discontent and bared her teeth at the youngster. Immediately the filly responded, it was her natural instinct. She lashed out, her eyes as white as the glare on water. The herd bunched together behind The Beast, watching with apprehension as the scene unfolded. Suddenly Thibaut stepped in.

'Come on,' he murmured, making reassuring noises, 'Leave it. Come on.'

The filly relaxed and the tension fell away from

her taut muscles. She pushed her nose to the ground as The Beast assumed a martyred air.

'Come on Blanche,' Thibaut whispered to the filly and she moved away.

'Hang on!' exclaimed Quentin, 'She's not coming with us in that state! She's a troublemaker! A problem horse! We've got a hard enough job ahead of us without some unpredictable, over-excitable yearling causing mayhem!'

Thibaut knew Quentin had a point but he was reluctant to leave Blanche.

'Well what do you want me to do?' he questioned, 'Just release her? She'll never survive out there on her own! I'll look after her!'

As if to prove a point he laid his hand on her nose. Blanche flung her head in the air and, with her ears flat out against her skull, she backed into the group. They scattered, squealing. Quentin laid a hand on Blanche's rump and she took off across the sedge, pink flamingos rising with clattering wings as she splashed through the water. The sunlight made a spectrum of the cascade of water that rose and re-settled in her wake. Thibaut felt a strange sadness for her as he watched her go. It was midday and the hot sun was beating down on his neck. He watched the salmon flamingos against the azure sky for a moment, then slapped his forehead as if to clear it. He reluctantly turned on his heel and re-mounted Anne-Marie.

The herd made slow progress across the marshes and by the evening they arrived at their destination. This was where the herd was to be branded with the stamp of the man for whom Thibaut and Quentin worked. The boys corralled the horses and then turned in for the night. They slept in a makeshift wooden hut. It was bare and simple, yet adequate. Thibaut stayed outside for a while and watched the flamingos come in to roost. They were almost camouflaged against the pink stains on the darkening sky. Thibaut cast his eyes along the black strip of horizon, blanketed by patchwork sky. The crickets were beginning to chirp amongst the thyme and the herd was at ease.

Thibaut was just about to return to his hut when a brief flash of silver caught his eye. It was Blanche, her snowy coat burnished silver by the rising moon, which was as yellow as a round of brie. He watched her as she watched the herd, ears pricked, anticipating the need to flee. Thibaut out-stretched his hand and whickered softly to her. Her ears swivelled and she threw up her head, eyes reflecting splinters of moonlight. Thibaut stayed where he was and eventually she softened and walked towards him. Her gait was loose and long, she didn't hurry. The only things that betrayed her tensions were her ears, still standing like stiff sentries on top of her head. Blanche pushed her nose into Thibaut's proffered hand and sniffed back gently. Thibaut stroked her nose and then turned back to the hut, her heart dancing in his chest.

The boy and beast continued to meet in this elusive fashion for a number of days. Sunday came and went, and after a day of rest spent with his mind working overtime, Thibaut knew what he had to do. Evening came and the boys crashed out. It was their last night in the hut before they hit the road again. It was the markets of Orange they headed for tomorrow, and the three nights spent in the saddle en route would be sleepless and uncomfortable. It was a matter of minutes before Thibaut heard Quentin's snores. He crept through the dark hut and over the threshold. The still night air was heady with the scent of herbs. Their fragrance stupefied him and he blinked heavily. Crickets relayed their monotonous calls in the undergrowth, their shrill cries splintering the silence. Thibaut smiled and held out his hand to the ghostly white figure of Blanche. As he took a step forward a soft voice came from behind.

'You've got to stop this, Thibaut.'
Startled, Thibaut spun round. He hadn't noticed Quentin watching him.

'She's better now!' Thibaut protested as Quentin took his arm.

''No,' whispered Quentin. 'She's practically tame, the herd will never accept her now.'

'Well I'll keep her!' exclaimed Thibaut excitedly.

'You know as well as anyone that we can't afford to pay to keep another horse,' Quentin reminded him forcefully.

'Just give her a chance!' pleaded Thibaut. 'Please!'

Quentin knew he couldn't deal with Thibaut while he was so worked up so he turned and steered him back to the hut. With the new light that morning would bring, he figured Thibaut might see things differently.

The next day Blanche was re-introduced to the herd. The sun hid its face behind a cloud as it watched the resulting turmoil. The vicious catfight for precedence between Blanche and The Beast had turned into a full-scale riot and it took many frantic minutes of dodging flying hooves before Thibaut and Quentin managed to regain control of the herd. Afterwards, blood and tears mingled and trickled down Thibaut's face. The salty drops of sadness and pain splashed on the ground and fell into the bucket of warm water that he was using to clean the wounds of the other horses in the herd. After the fight, Blanche had disappeared like the elusive butterfly that danced mockingly around Thibaut's feet. He felt like a failure. Quentin had been right again. Now The Beast was crippled and the herd was tense and jittery. They would not be able to travel today. Blanche was gone, but Thibaut and Quentin knew she would be back.

That night Quentin watched from the fence of the corral as Blanche came and greeted Thibaut for the last time. Thibaut stroked her nose. It felt like velvet to his work-worn hands. He saw his tearful eyes reflected in the caliginous pools of her eyes and with a sharp slap on her quarters, he sent her away.

But she came back to him, her puzzled face enquiring. She nosed at the pockets of his dusty cropped jeans expectantly. Thibaut knew what he had to do. He bravely raised the stick with trembling arms, and with one harsh blow all the relentless hours of work, love, and the strong bond between the animal and the boy, were shattered.

Blanche whipped round like a hurricane, mane flying. Her razor sharp hooves beat against Thibaut's thigh, ripping the faded denim that shrouded them. The blood pooled at his feet but he didn't feel the pain. He sank to the ground. Blanche's high-pitched scream resounded in his ears as if it was a manic bell proclaiming his doom. He would never forget the fear and the hurt that poured from her soul to his as she had turned to flee. As he lowered his dust and tear-filled eyes he knew that she would never come back.

**THE DYSLEXIA
INSTITUTE**

For more information on dyslexia and the work
of the Dyslexia Institute visit their website
www.dyslexia-inst.org.uk

The Dyslexia Institute
Park House,
Wick Road,
Egham,
Surrey TW20 0HH
Tel. 01784 222300
Fax. 01784 222333